Cassandra

ANIMAL PSYCHIC #1

CASSANDRA STEPS OUT

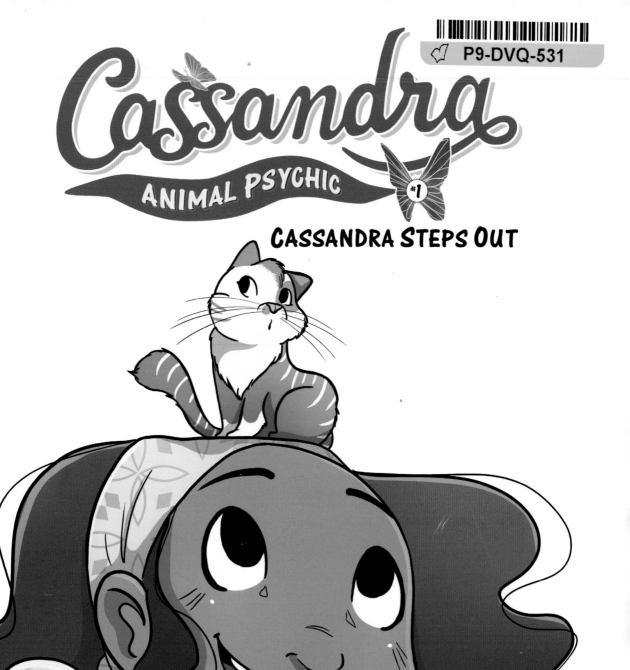

Isabelle Bottier
Hélène Canac

Graphic Universe™ • Minneapolis

A huge thank-you to Estelle and Isabelle for this project, which fits me 100 percent! It's such a pleasure to work with you! Thanks also for my Choupi for encouraging me during the creation of this volume and to Agnes for making Juliet's bedroom so wonderfully beautiful. Victor, Daphne, Martin, this album is for you . . . once you can read!

—H.C.

A big thank-you to Estelle for her kindness and to Hélène for creating such a lovely Cassandra. And a big treat to the real Dolly, who continues to live in the heart of her master.

—I.B.

Story by Isabelle Bottier
Illustrations by Hélène Canac
Coloring by Drac

First American edition published in 2019 by Graphic Universe™

Published by arrangement with Steinkis Groupe

Cassandra prend son envol © 2017 by Jungle

Translation by Norwyn MacTire

English translation copyright © 2019 by Lerner Publishing Group, Inc.

Graphic Universe™ is a trademark of Lerner Publishing Group, Inc.

Graphic Universe™
A division of Lerner Publishing Group, Inc.
241 First Avenue North
Minneapolis, MN 55401 USA

For reading levels and more information, look up this title at www.lernerbooks.com.

Main body text set in Andy Std 9/10.5.
Typeface provided by Monotype Typography.

Library of Congress Cataloging-in-Publication Data

Names: Bottier, Isabelle, author. | Canac, Hélène, illustrator. | MacTyre, Norwyn, translator.
Title: Cassandra steps out / Isabelle Bottier ; Helene Canac ; coloring by Drac ; translation by Norwyn MacTyre.
Other titles: Cassandra prend son envol. French.
Description: First American edition. | Minneapolis : Graphic Universe, 2019. | Series: Cassandra, animal psychic ; book 1 | Summary: While struggling to cope with major changes in her life, fourteen-year-old Cassandra decides to help others by using her ability to see what animals are thinking, beginning with finding a lost cat.
Identifiers: LCCN 2018052142 (print) | LCCN 2018056241 (ebook) | ISBN 9781541561106 (eb pdf) | ISBN 9781541543973 (lb : alk. paper) | ISBN 9781541572836 (pb : alk. paper)
Subjects: LCSH: Graphic novels. | CYAC: Graphic novels. | Psychic ability—Fiction. | Human-animal communication—Fiction. | Change (Psychology)—Fiction. | Family life—Fiction.
Classification: LCC PZ7.7.B675 (ebook) | LCC PZ7.7.B675 Cas 2019 (print) | DDC 741.5/944—dc23

LC record available at https://lccn.loc.gov/2018052142

Manufactured in the United States of America
1-45426-39683-2/8/2019

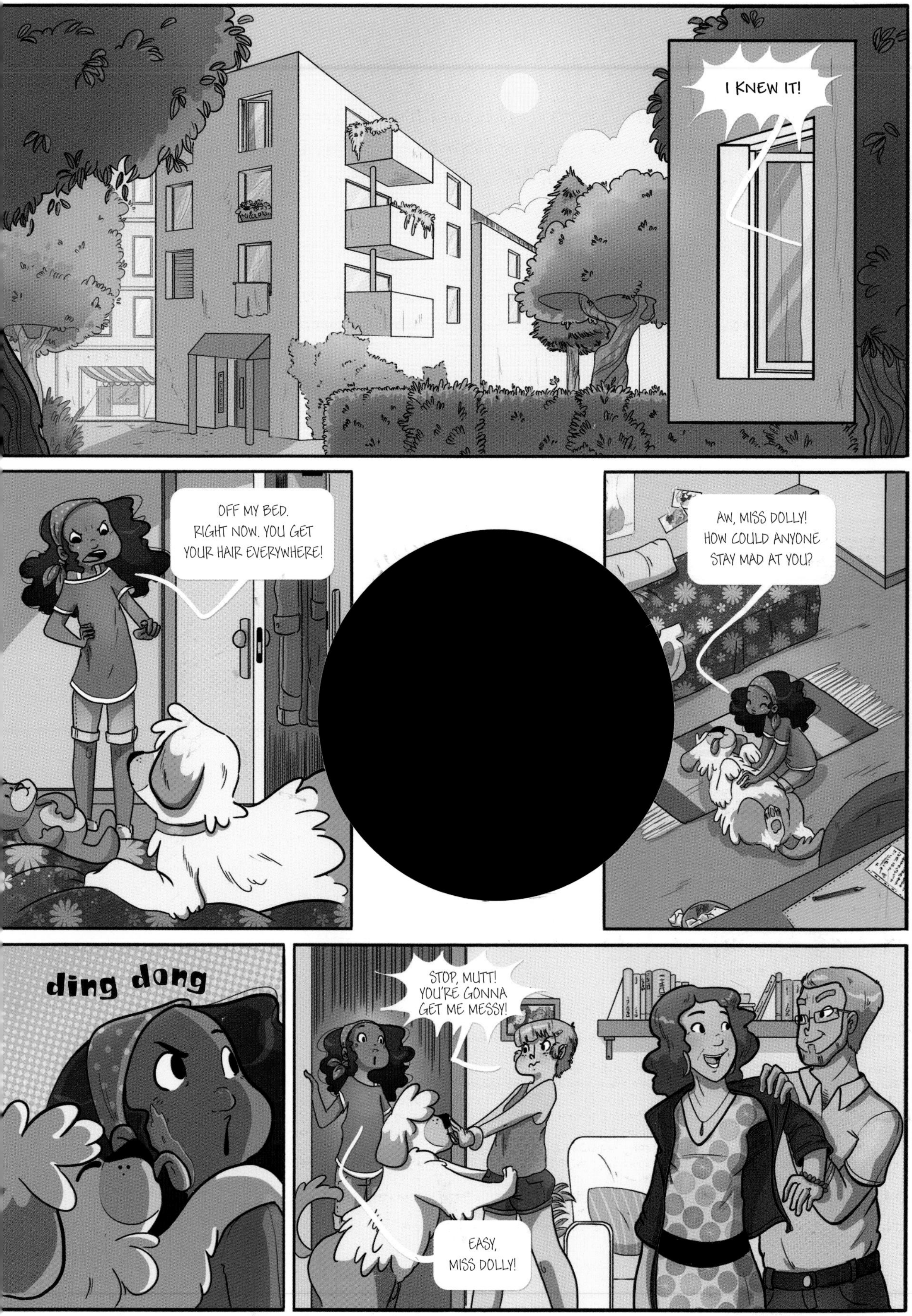
I KNEW IT!
OFF MY BED. RIGHT NOW. YOU GET YOUR HAIR EVERYWHERE!
AW, MISS DOLLY! HOW COULD ANYONE STAY MAD AT YOU?
ding dong
STOP, MUTT! YOU'RE GONNA GET ME MESSY!
EASY, MISS DOLLY!

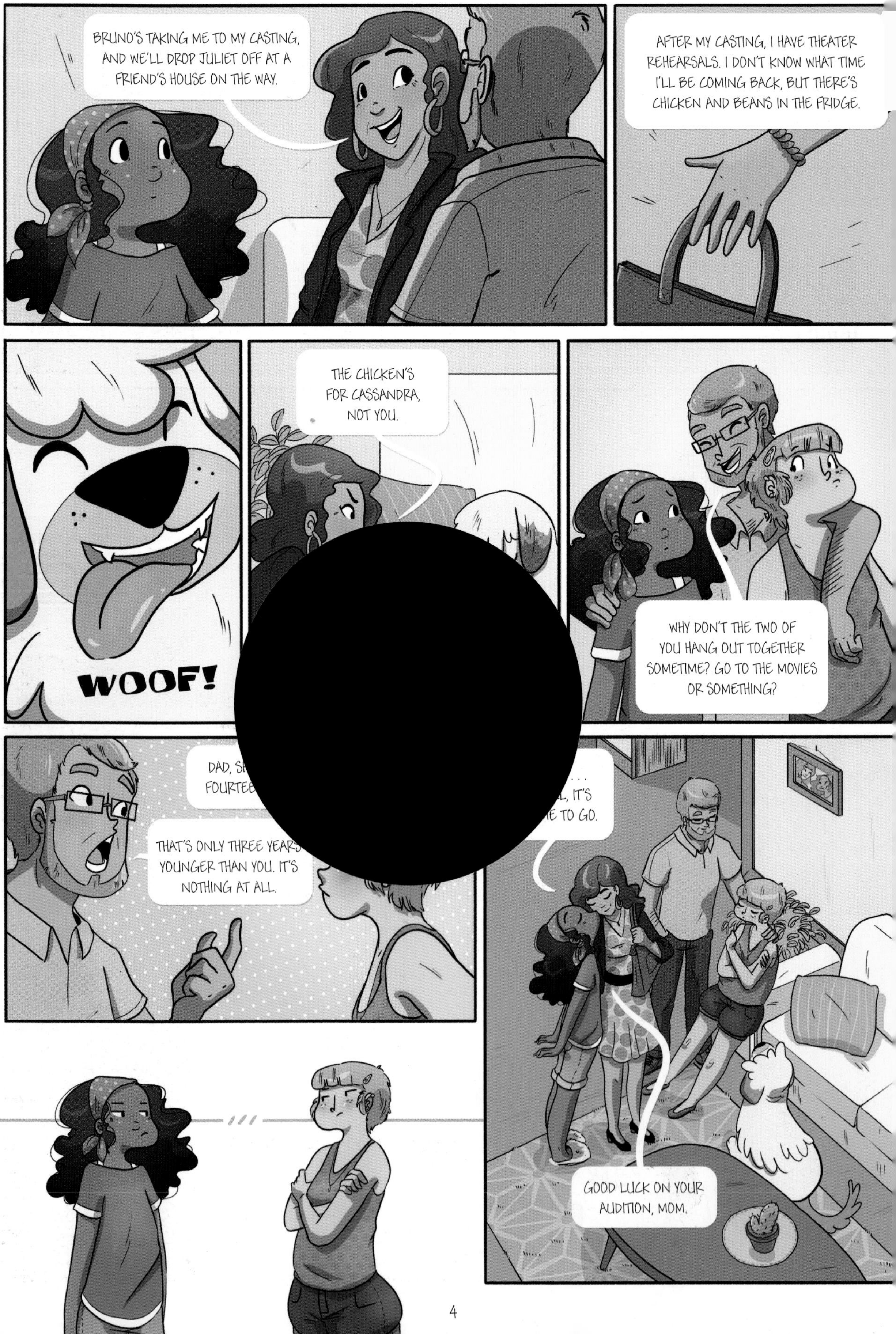
BRUNO'S TAKING ME TO MY CASTING, AND WE'LL DROP JULIET OFF AT A FRIEND'S HOUSE ON THE WAY.
AFTER MY CASTING, I HAVE THEATER REHEARSALS. I DON'T KNOW WHAT TIME I'LL BE COMING BACK, BUT THERE'S CHICKEN AND BEANS IN THE FRIDGE.
WOOF!
THE CHICKEN'S FOR CASSANDRA, NOT YOU.
WHY DON'T THE TWO OF YOU HANG OUT TOGETHER SOMETIME? GO TO THE MOVIES OR SOMETHING?
DAD, [redacted]
THAT'S ONLY THREE YEARS YOUNGER THAN YOU. IT'S NOTHING AT ALL.
[redacted] IT'S [redacted] TO GO.
GOOD LUCK ON YOUR AUDITION, MOM.

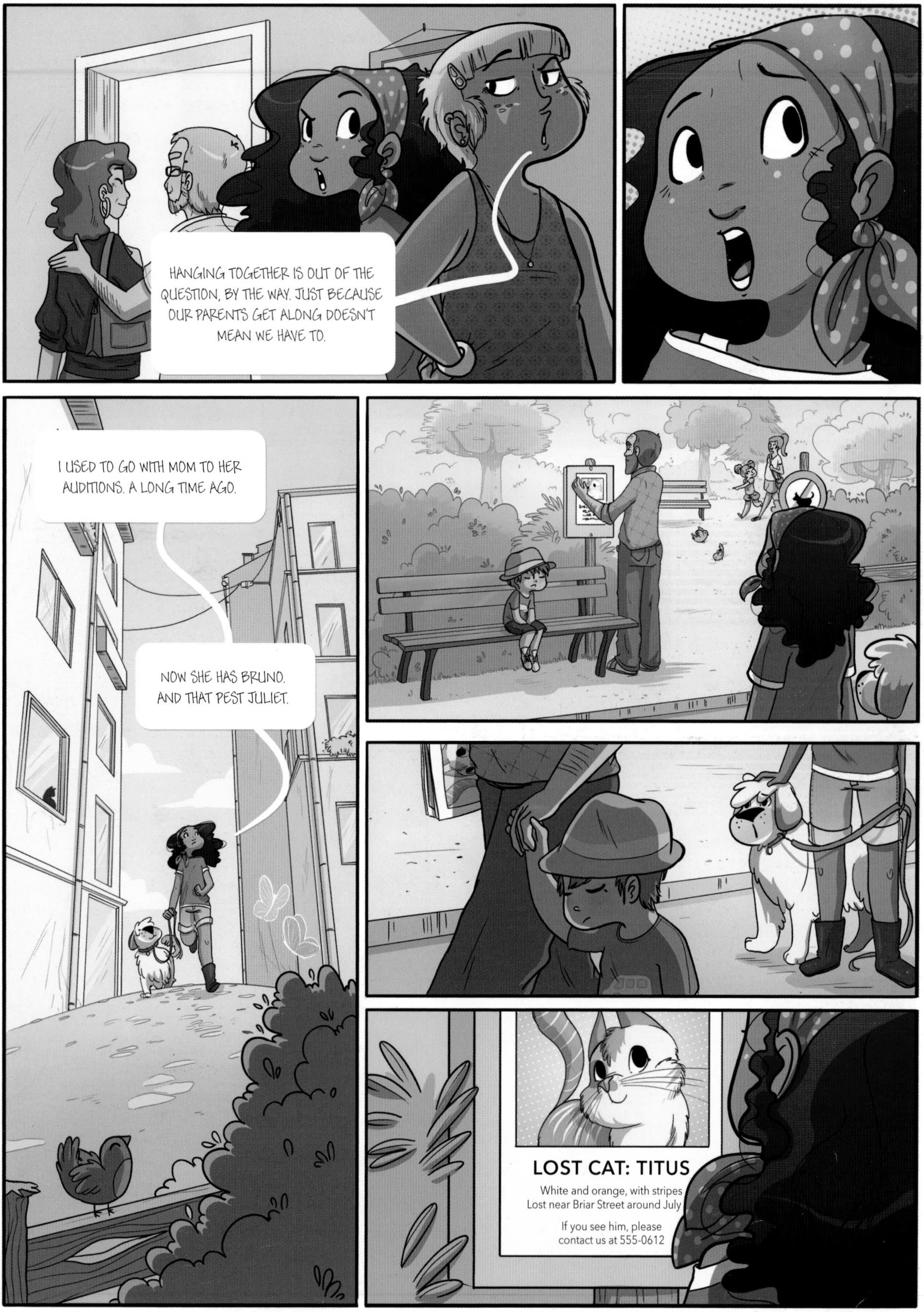
HANGING TOGETHER IS OUT OF THE QUESTION, BY THE WAY. JUST BECAUSE OUR PARENTS GET ALONG DOESN'T MEAN WE HAVE TO.
I USED TO GO WITH MOM TO HER AUDITIONS. A LONG TIME AGO.
NOW SHE HAS BRUNO. AND THAT PEST JULIET.
LOST CAT: TITUS
White and orange, with stripes
Lost near Briar Street around July
If you see him, please contact us at 555-0612

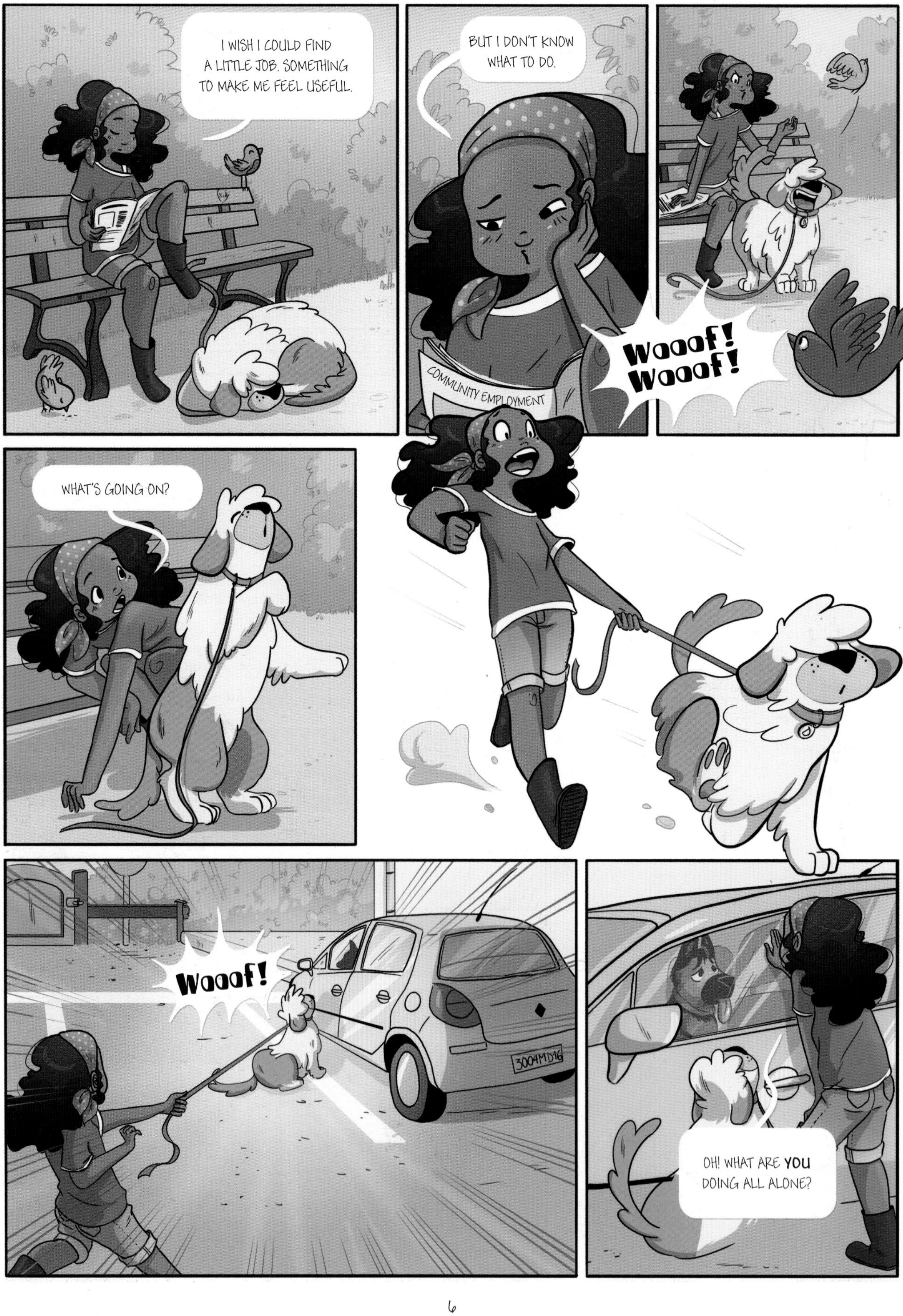

I WISH I COULD FIND A LITTLE JOB. SOMETHING TO MAKE ME FEEL USEFUL.
BUT I DON'T KNOW WHAT TO DO.
COMMUNITY EMPLOYMENT
Wooof! Wooof!
WHAT'S GOING ON?
Wooof!
3004MD16
OH! WHAT ARE **YOU** DOING ALL ALONE?

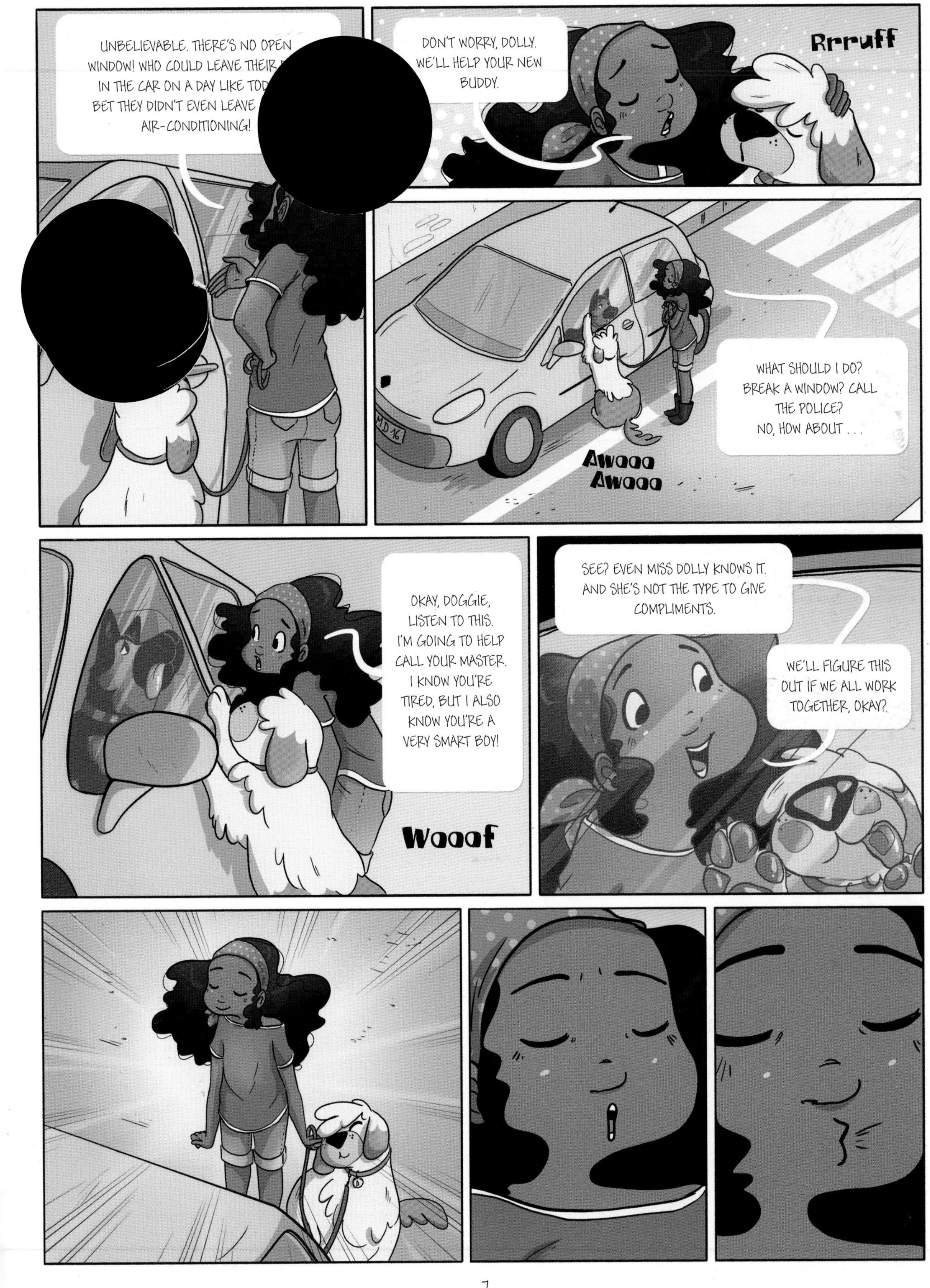
UNBELIEVABLE. THERE'S NO OPEN WINDOW! WHO COULD LEAVE THEIR [redacted] IN THE CAR ON A DAY LIKE TOD[redacted] BET THEY DIDN'T EVEN LEAVE [redacted] AIR-CONDITIONING!
DON'T WORRY, DOLLY. WE'LL HELP YOUR NEW BUDDY.
Rrruff
WHAT SHOULD I DO? BREAK A WINDOW? CALL THE POLICE? NO, HOW ABOUT . . .
MD 16
Awooo Awooo
OKAY, DOGGIE, LISTEN TO THIS. I'M GOING TO HELP CALL YOUR MASTER. I KNOW YOU'RE TIRED, BUT I ALSO KNOW YOU'RE A VERY SMART BOY!
Wooof
SEE? EVEN MISS DOLLY KNOWS IT. AND SHE'S NOT THE TYPE TO GIVE COMPLIMENTS.
WE'LL FIGURE THIS OUT IF WE ALL WORK TOGETHER, OKAY?

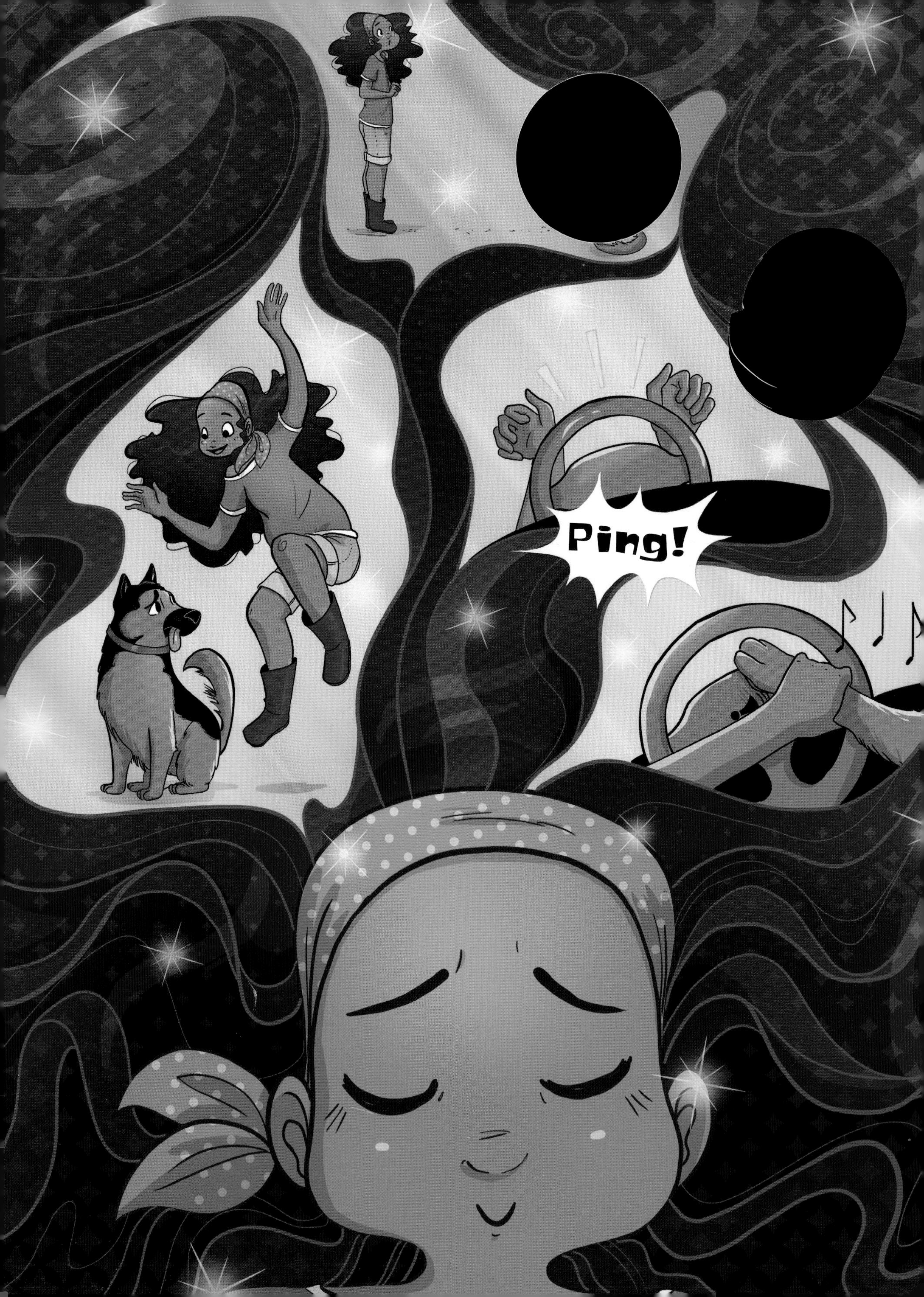
Ping!

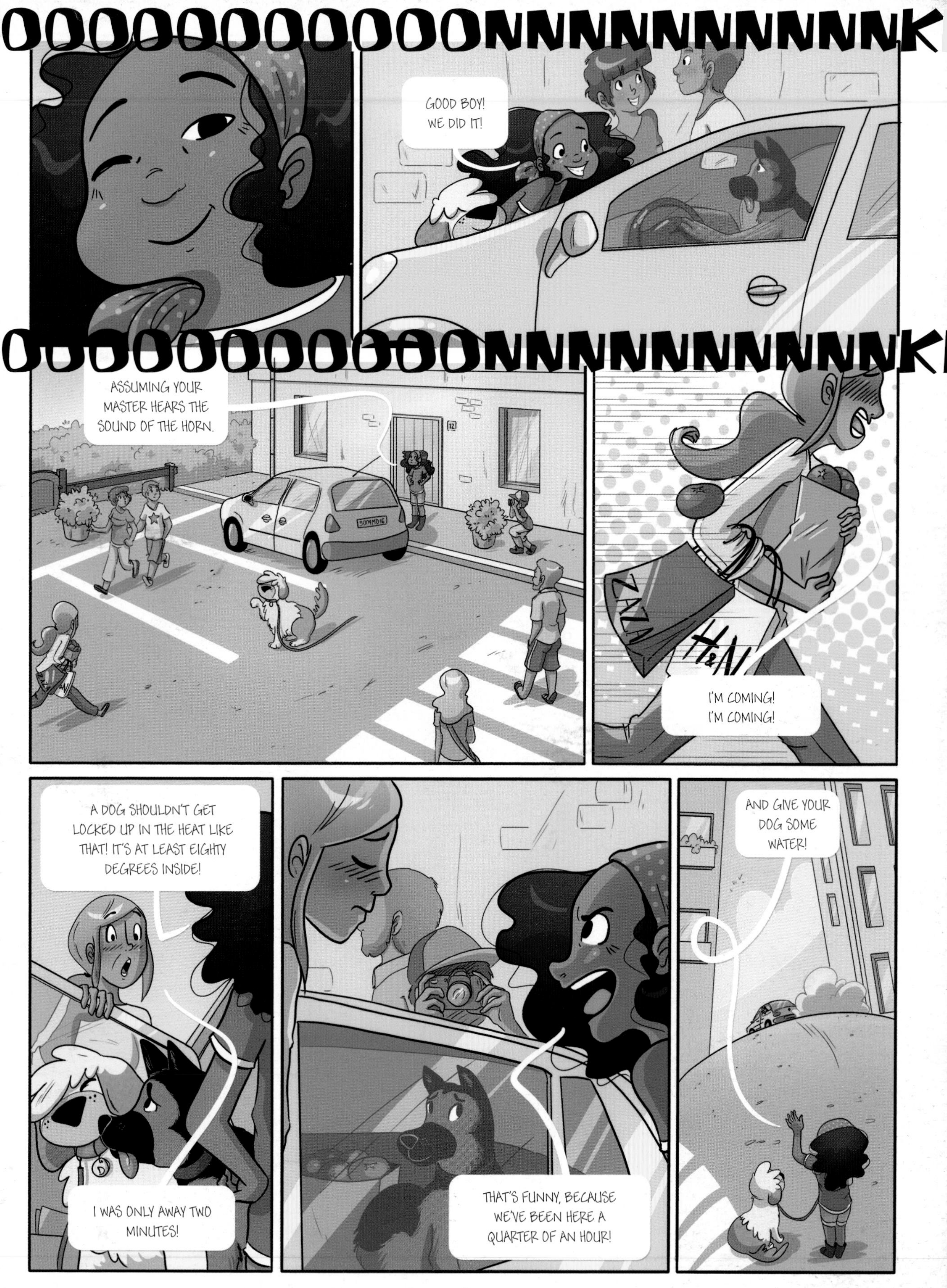
OOOOOOOOOOOOONNNNNNNNNNNNK
GOOD BOY! WE DID IT!
OOOOOOOOOOOOONNNNNNNNNNNNK
ASSUMING YOUR MASTER HEARS THE SOUND OF THE HORN.
I'M COMING! I'M COMING!
A DOG SHOULDN'T GET LOCKED UP IN THE HEAT LIKE THAT! IT'S AT LEAST EIGHTY DEGREES INSIDE!
I WAS ONLY AWAY TWO MINUTES!
THAT'S FUNNY, BECAUSE WE'VE BEEN HERE A QUARTER OF AN HOUR!
AND GIVE YOUR DOG SOME WATER!

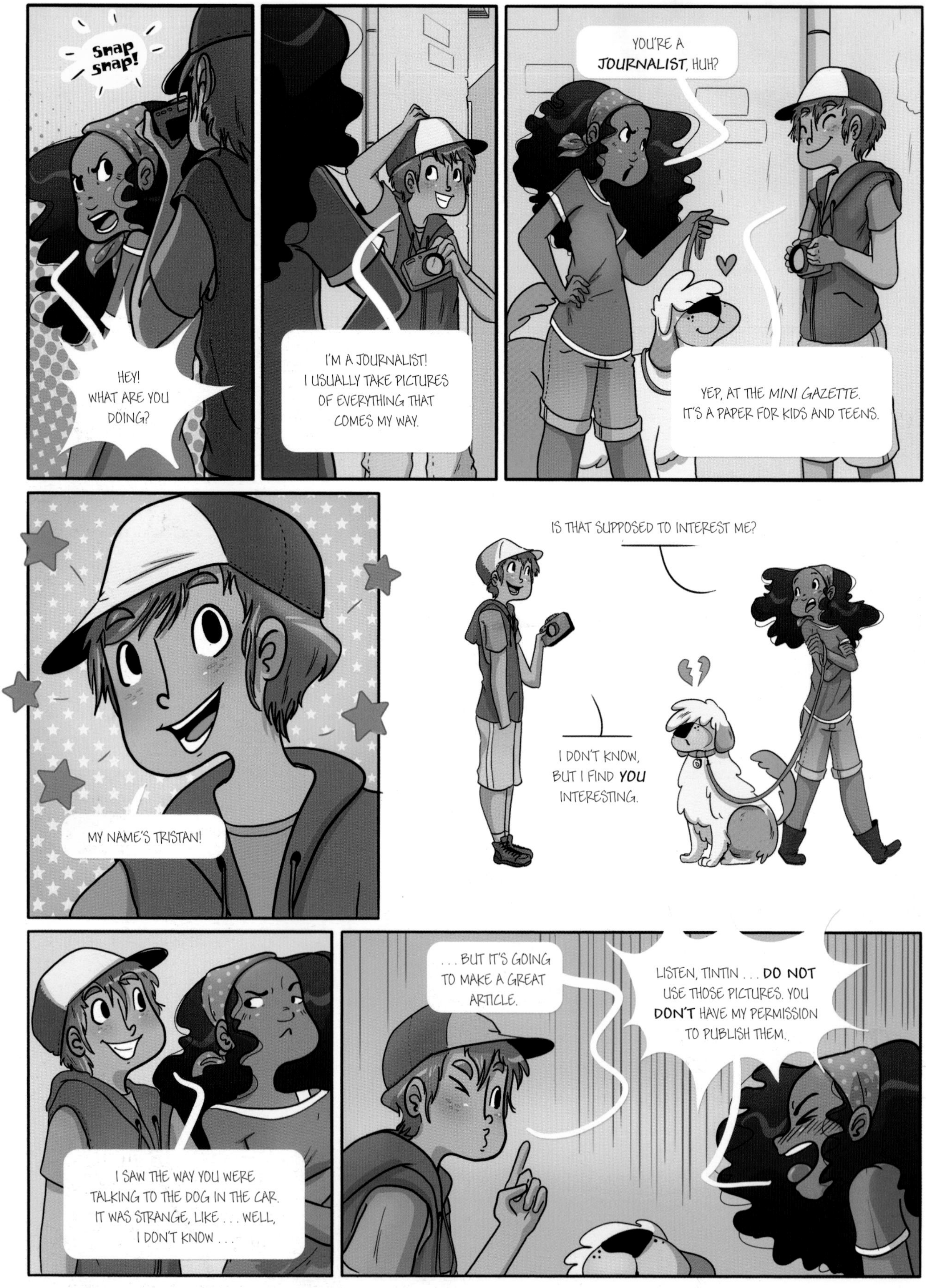
Snap snap!
HEY! WHAT ARE YOU DOING?
I'M A JOURNALIST! I USUALLY TAKE PICTURES OF EVERYTHING THAT COMES MY WAY.
YOU'RE A **JOURNALIST**, HUH?
YEP, AT THE *MINI GAZETTE*. IT'S A PAPER FOR KIDS AND TEENS.
MY NAME'S TRISTAN!
IS THAT SUPPOSED TO INTEREST ME?
I DON'T KNOW, BUT I FIND **YOU** INTERESTING.
I SAW THE WAY YOU WERE TALKING TO THE DOG IN THE CAR. IT WAS STRANGE, LIKE . . . WELL, I DON'T KNOW . . .
. . . BUT IT'S GOING TO MAKE A GREAT ARTICLE.
LISTEN, TINTIN . . . **DO NOT** USE THOSE PICTURES. YOU **DON'T** HAVE MY PERMISSION TO PUBLISH THEM.

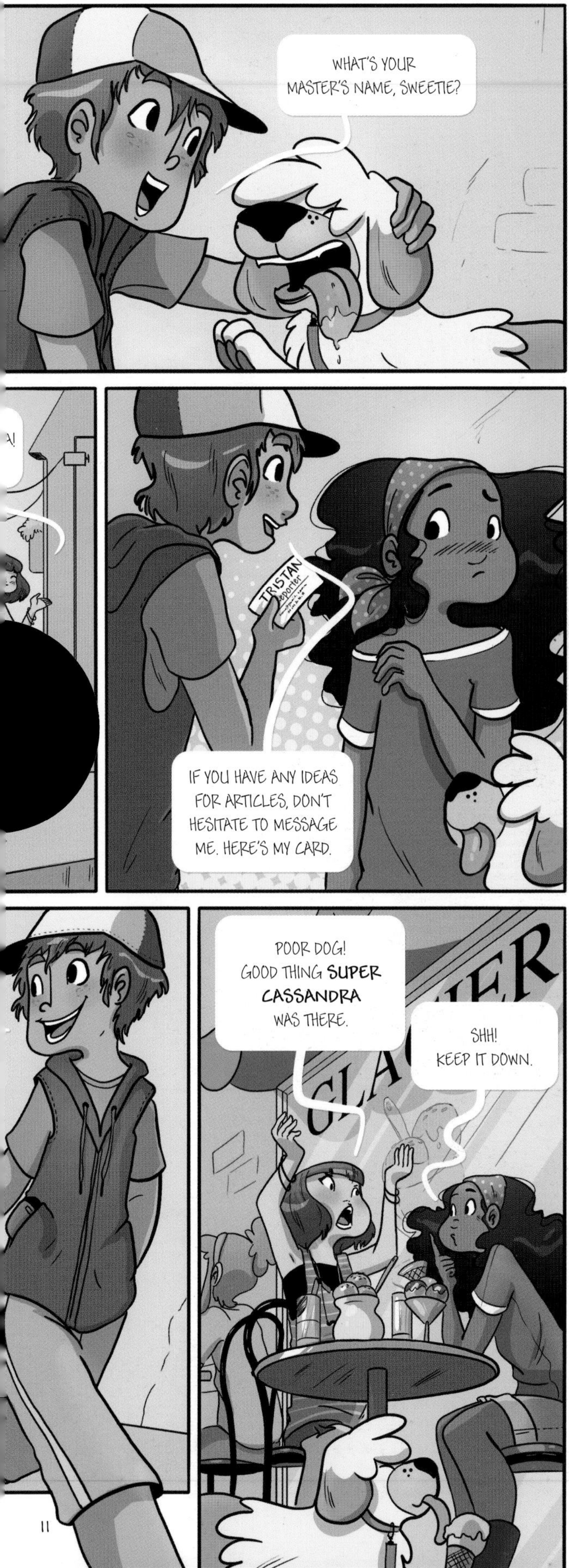
WHAT'S YOUR MASTER'S NAME, SWEETIE?
TRISTAN
Reporter
IF YOU HAVE ANY IDEAS FOR ARTICLES, DON'T HESITATE TO MESSAGE ME. HERE'S MY CARD.
POOR DOG! GOOD THING **SUPER CASSANDRA** WAS THERE.
SHH! KEEP IT DOWN.

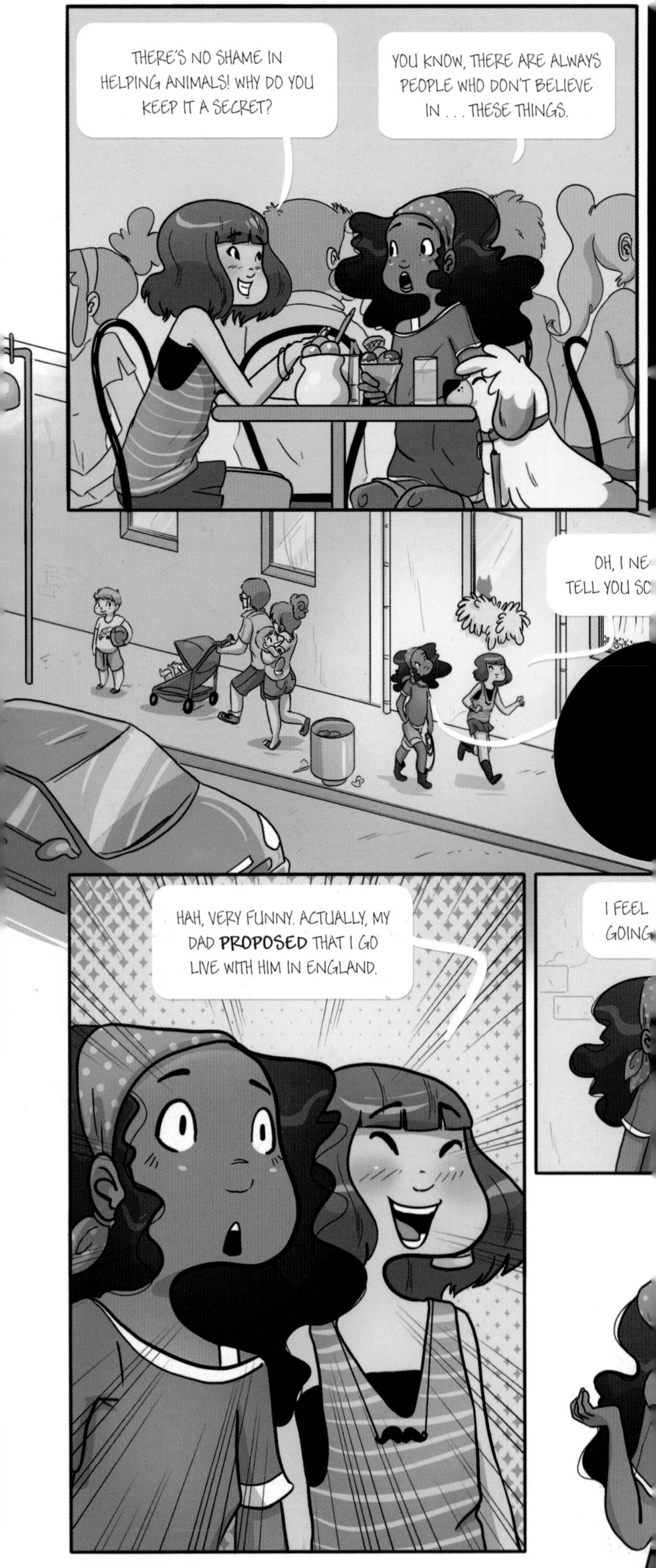
THERE'S NO SHAME IN HELPING ANIMALS! WHY DO YOU KEEP IT A SECRET?
YOU KNOW, THERE ARE ALWAYS PEOPLE WHO DON'T BELIEVE IN . . . THESE THINGS.
OH, I NE TELL YOU SC
HAH, VERY FUNNY. ACTUALLY, MY DAD **PROPOSED** THAT I GO LIVE WITH HIM IN ENGLAND.
I FEEL GOING

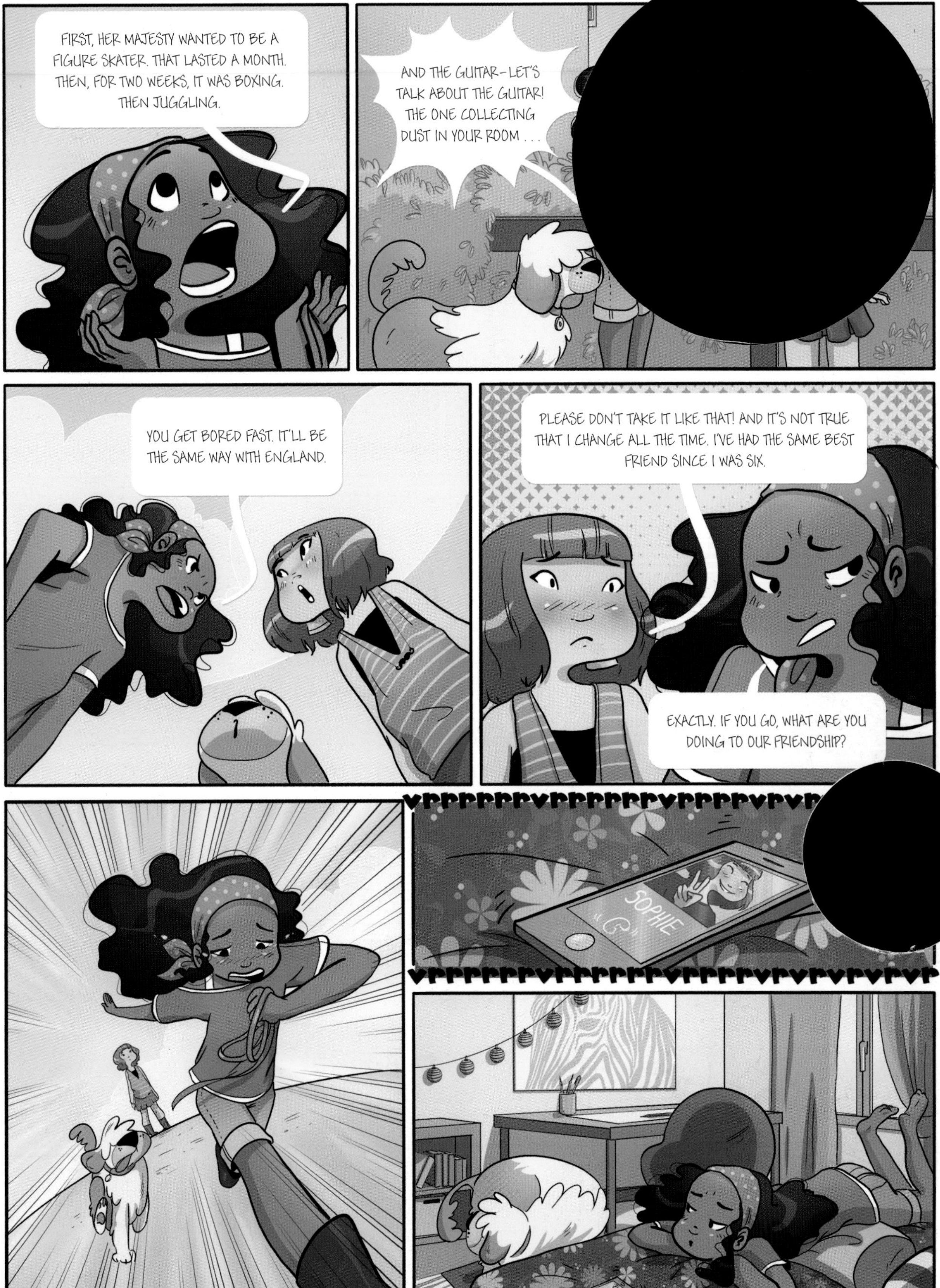
FIRST, HER MAJESTY WANTED TO BE A FIGURE SKATER. THAT LASTED A MONTH. THEN, FOR TWO WEEKS, IT WAS BOXING. THEN JUGGLING.
AND THE GUITAR—LET'S TALK ABOUT THE GUITAR! THE ONE COLLECTING DUST IN YOUR ROOM . . .
YOU GET BORED FAST. IT'LL BE THE SAME WAY WITH ENGLAND.
PLEASE DON'T TAKE IT LIKE THAT! AND IT'S NOT TRUE THAT I CHANGE ALL THE TIME. I'VE HAD THE SAME BEST FRIEND SINCE I WAS SIX.
EXACTLY. IF YOU GO, WHAT ARE YOU DOING TO OUR FRIENDSHIP?
SOPHIE

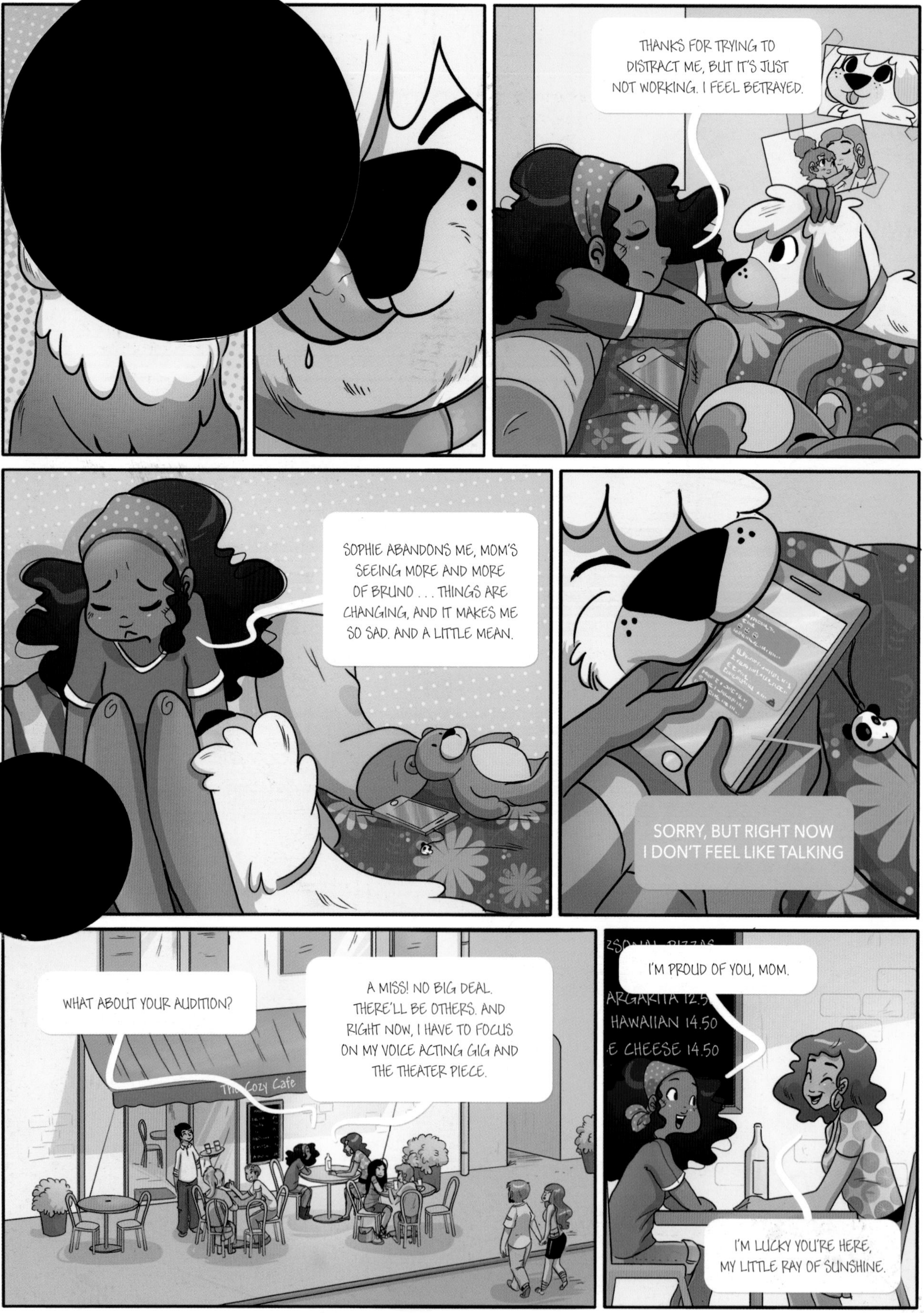
THANKS FOR TRYING TO DISTRACT ME, BUT IT'S JUST NOT WORKING. I FEEL BETRAYED.
SOPHIE ABANDONS ME, MOM'S SEEING MORE AND MORE OF BRUNO . . . THINGS ARE CHANGING, AND IT MAKES ME SO SAD. AND A LITTLE MEAN.
SORRY, BUT RIGHT NOW I DON'T FEEL LIKE TALKING
WHAT ABOUT YOUR AUDITION?
A MISS! NO BIG DEAL. THERE'LL BE OTHERS. AND RIGHT NOW, I HAVE TO FOCUS ON MY VOICE ACTING GIG AND THE THEATER PIECE.
The Cozy Cafe
I'M PROUD OF YOU, MOM.
HAWAIIAN 14.50
I'M LUCKY YOU'RE HERE, MY LITTLE RAY OF SUNSHINE.

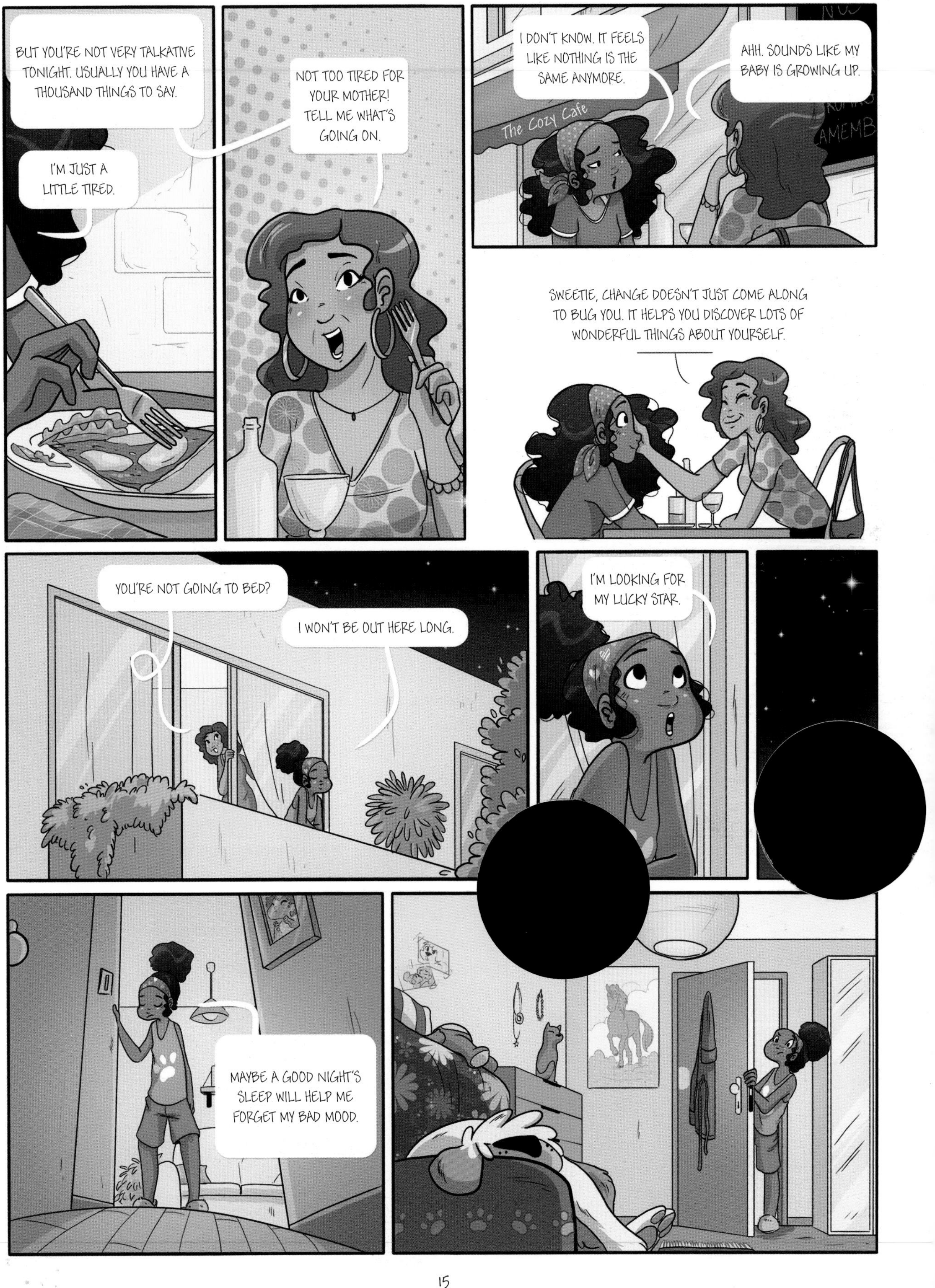

BUT YOU'RE NOT VERY TALKATIVE TONIGHT. USUALLY YOU HAVE A THOUSAND THINGS TO SAY.
I'M JUST A LITTLE TIRED.
NOT TOO TIRED FOR YOUR MOTHER! TELL ME WHAT'S GOING ON.
I DON'T KNOW. IT FEELS LIKE NOTHING IS THE SAME ANYMORE.
The Cozy Cafe
AHH. SOUNDS LIKE MY BABY IS GROWING UP.
SWEETIE, CHANGE DOESN'T JUST COME ALONG TO BUG YOU. IT HELPS YOU DISCOVER LOTS OF WONDERFUL THINGS ABOUT YOURSELF.
YOU'RE NOT GOING TO BED?
I WON'T BE OUT HERE LONG.
I'M LOOKING FOR MY LUCKY STAR.
MAYBE A GOOD NIGHT'S SLEEP WILL HELP ME FORGET MY BAD MOOD.

YOU'RE A HEAVY SLEEPER, GIRL.

GRRROO GRR ON GRR ON GRR OO

WE CAN **TOTALLY** COUNT ON YOU WHEN A BURGLAR SHOWS UP.

8:15

0 messages

WHOA, WHAT AN AMAZING BUTTERFLY!

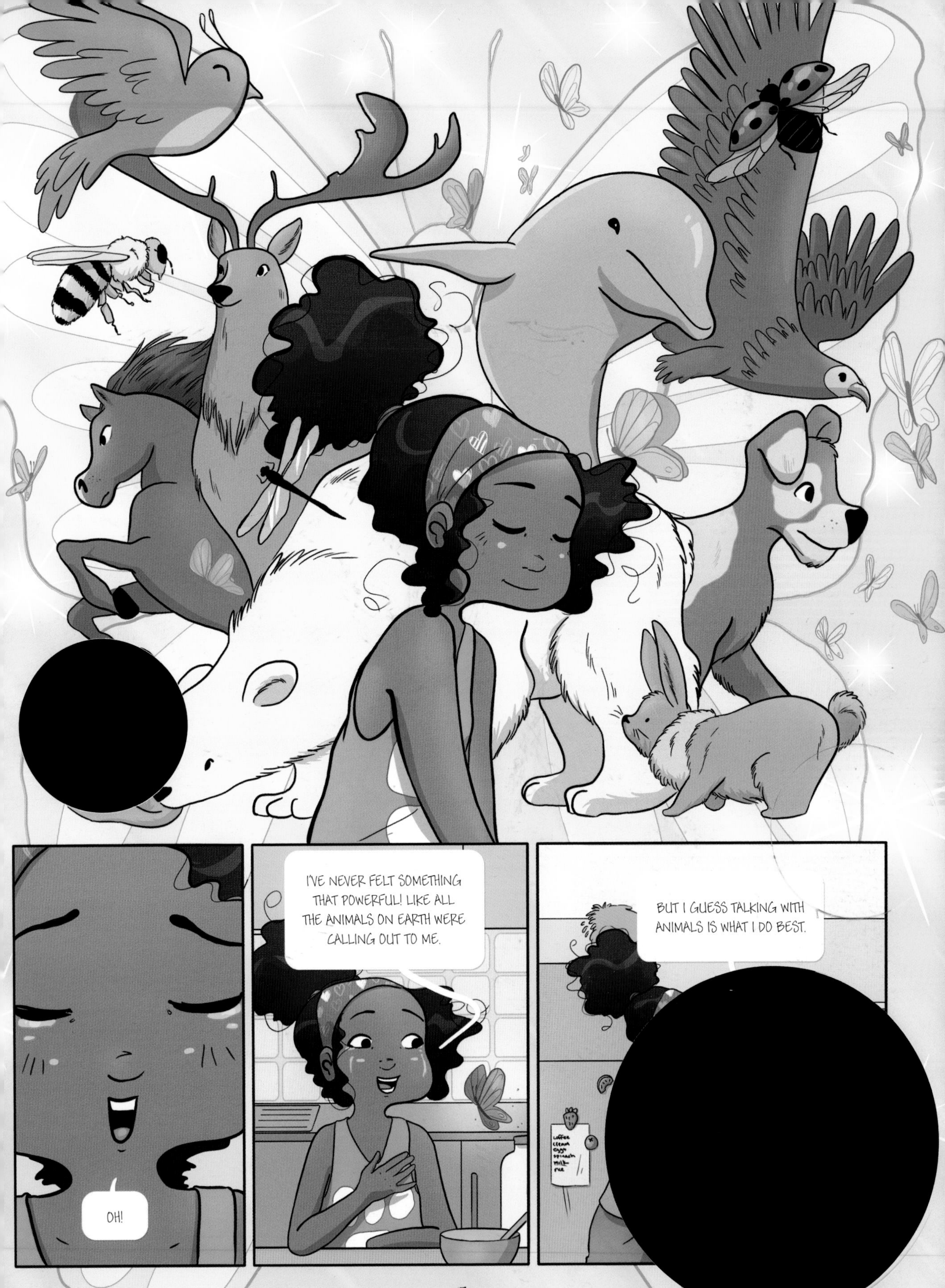
OH!
I'VE NEVER FELT SOMETHING THAT POWERFUL! LIKE ALL THE ANIMALS ON EARTH WERE CALLING OUT TO ME.
BUT I GUESS TALKING WITH ANIMALS IS WHAT I DO BEST.

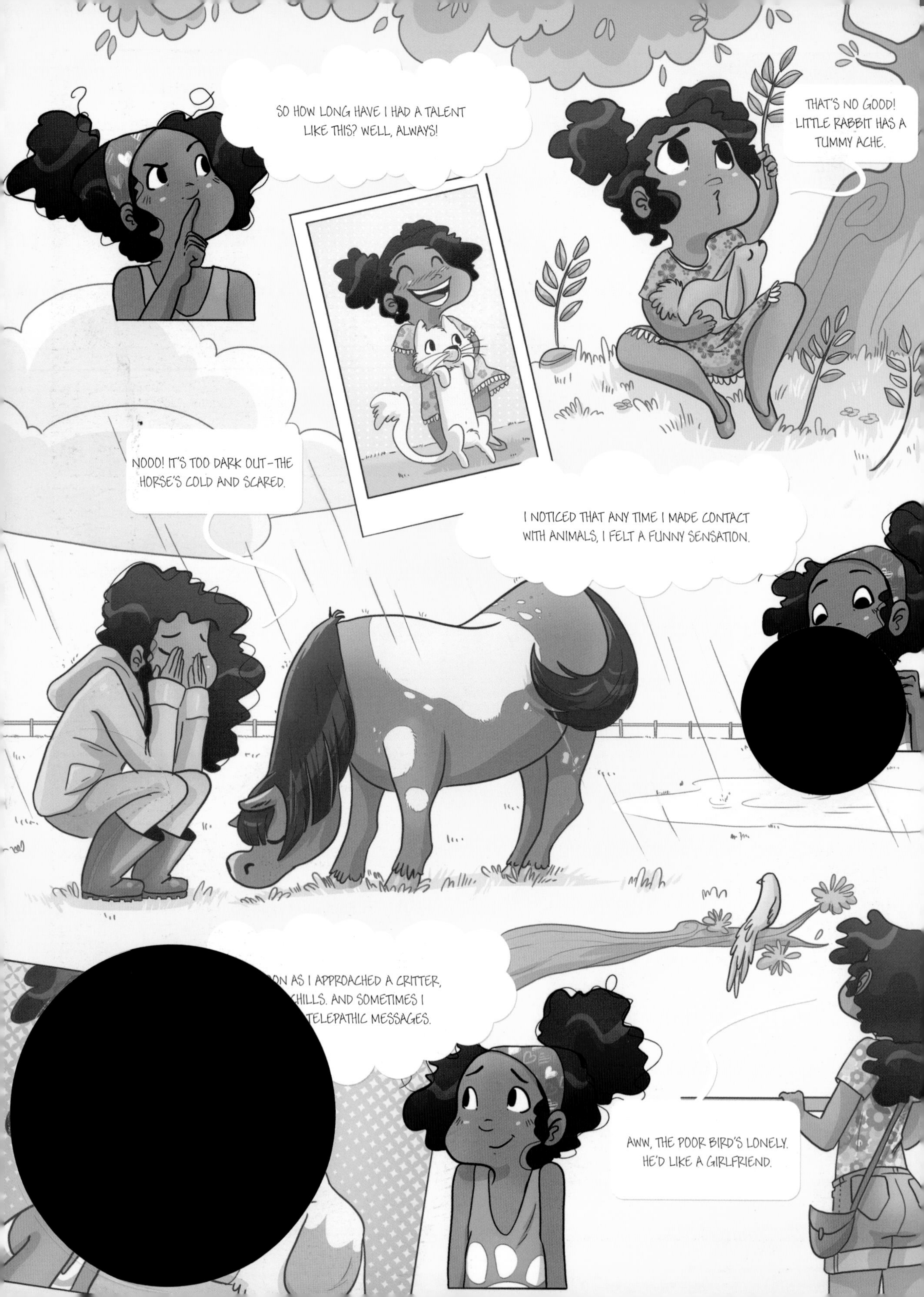
SO HOW LONG HAVE I HAD A TALENT LIKE THIS? WELL, ALWAYS!
THAT'S NO GOOD! LITTLE RABBIT HAS A TUMMY ACHE.
NOOO! IT'S TOO DARK OUT—THE HORSE'S COLD AND SCARED.
I NOTICED THAT ANY TIME I MADE CONTACT WITH ANIMALS, I FELT A FUNNY SENSATION.
[redacted]ON AS I APPROACHED A CRITTER, [redacted] CHILLS. AND SOMETIMES I [redacted] TELEPATHIC MESSAGES.
AWW, THE POOR BIRD'S LONELY. HE'D LIKE A GIRLFRIEND.

I CAN'T IGNORE THE ANIMALS' MESSAGES.

WOOF!

SOPHIE WAS RIGHT. WHO CARES WHAT OTHER PEOPLE THINK OF ME? IF I CAN DO SOME GOOD BY HELPING ANIMALS, THAT'S ALL THAT COUNTS.

ALTHOUGH I MISS SOPHIE ALREADY. WHAT'S SO GREAT ABOUT CHANGE IF IT TAKES AWAY SOMEONE YOU LOVE?

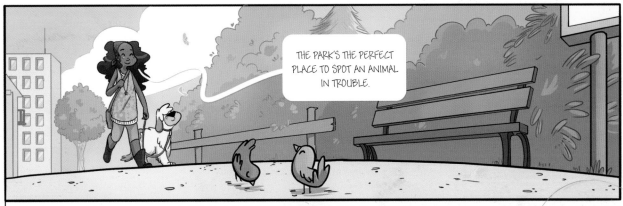

THE PARK'S THE PERFECT PLACE TO SPOT AN ANIMAL IN TROUBLE.

OH, THE BOY WHO LOST HIS CAT IS BACK.

WHAT IF . . . ?

LET'S GO. I'M NOT AFRAID TO BE MYSELF ANYMORE.

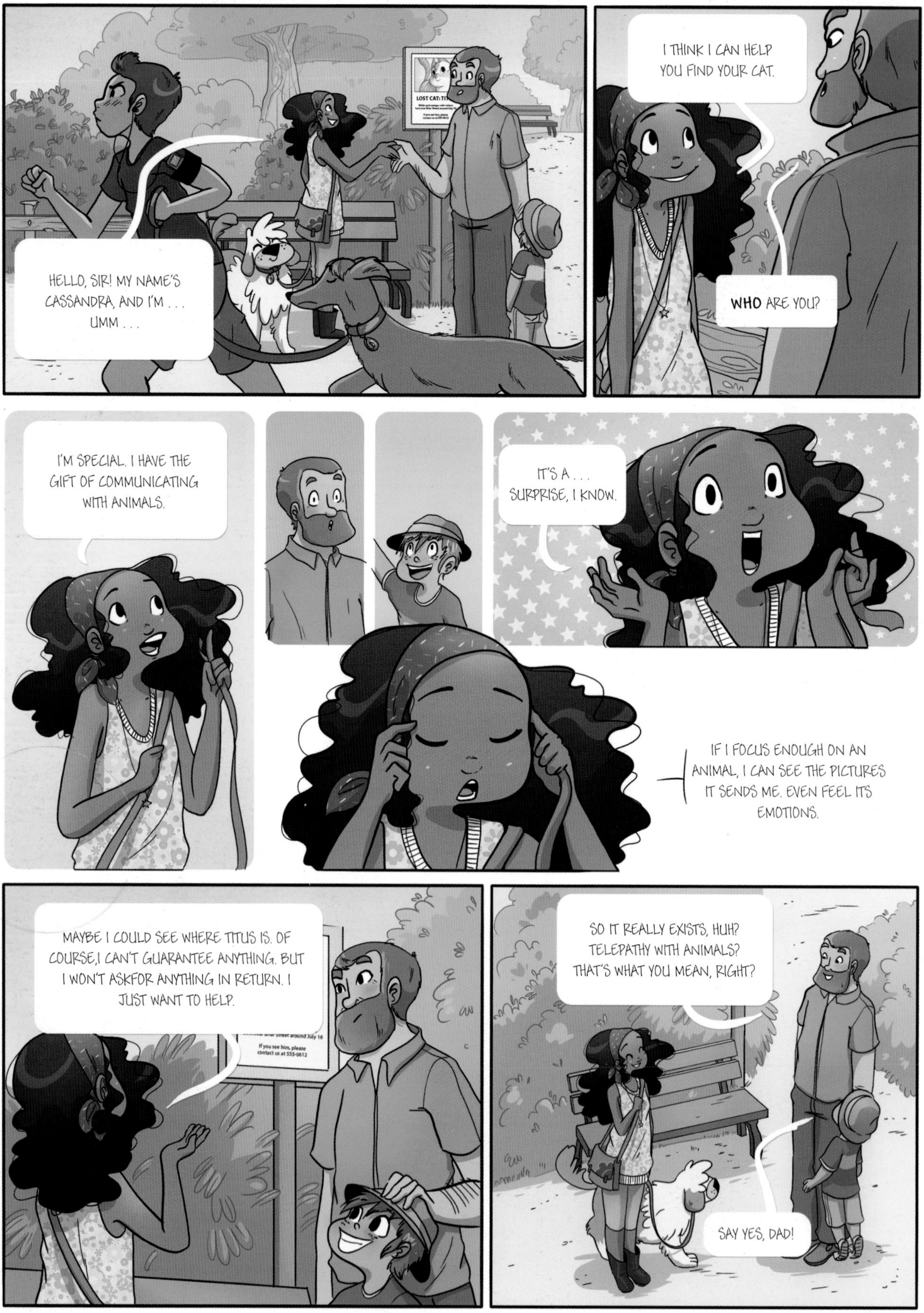
LOST CAT: TI
HELLO, SIR! MY NAME'S CASSANDRA, AND I'M . . . UMM . . .
I THINK I CAN HELP YOU FIND YOUR CAT.
WHO ARE YOU?
I'M SPECIAL. I HAVE THE GIFT OF COMMUNICATING WITH ANIMALS.
IT'S A . . . SURPRISE, I KNOW.
IF I FOCUS ENOUGH ON AN ANIMAL, I CAN SEE THE PICTURES IT SENDS ME. EVEN FEEL ITS EMOTIONS.
MAYBE I COULD SEE WHERE TITUS IS. OF COURSE,I CAN'T GUARANTEE ANYTHING. BUT I WON'T ASKFOR ANYTHING IN RETURN. I JUST WANT TO HELP.
If you see him, please contact us at 555-0612
SO IT REALLY EXISTS, HUH? TELEPATHY WITH ANIMALS? THAT'S WHAT YOU MEAN, RIGHT?
SAY YES, DAD!

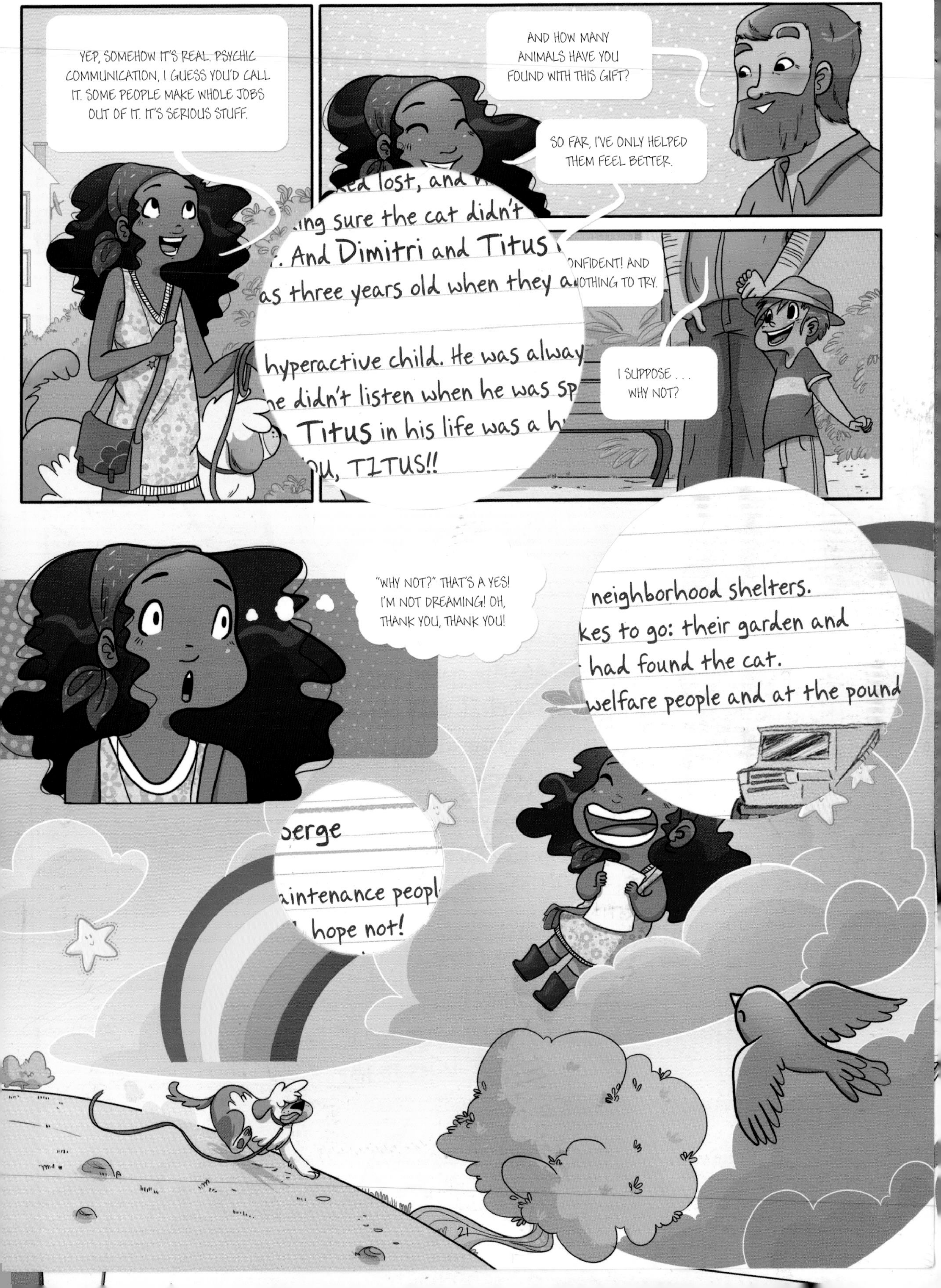
YEP, SOMEHOW IT'S REAL. PSYCHIC COMMUNICATION, I GUESS YOU'D CALL IT. SOME PEOPLE MAKE WHOLE JOBS OUT OF IT. IT'S SERIOUS STUFF.
AND HOW MANY ANIMALS HAVE YOU FOUND WITH THIS GIFT?
SO FAR, I'VE ONLY HELPED THEM FEEL BETTER.
I SUPPOSE . . . WHY NOT?
"WHY NOT?" THAT'S A YES! I'M NOT DREAMING! OH, THANK YOU, THANK YOU!

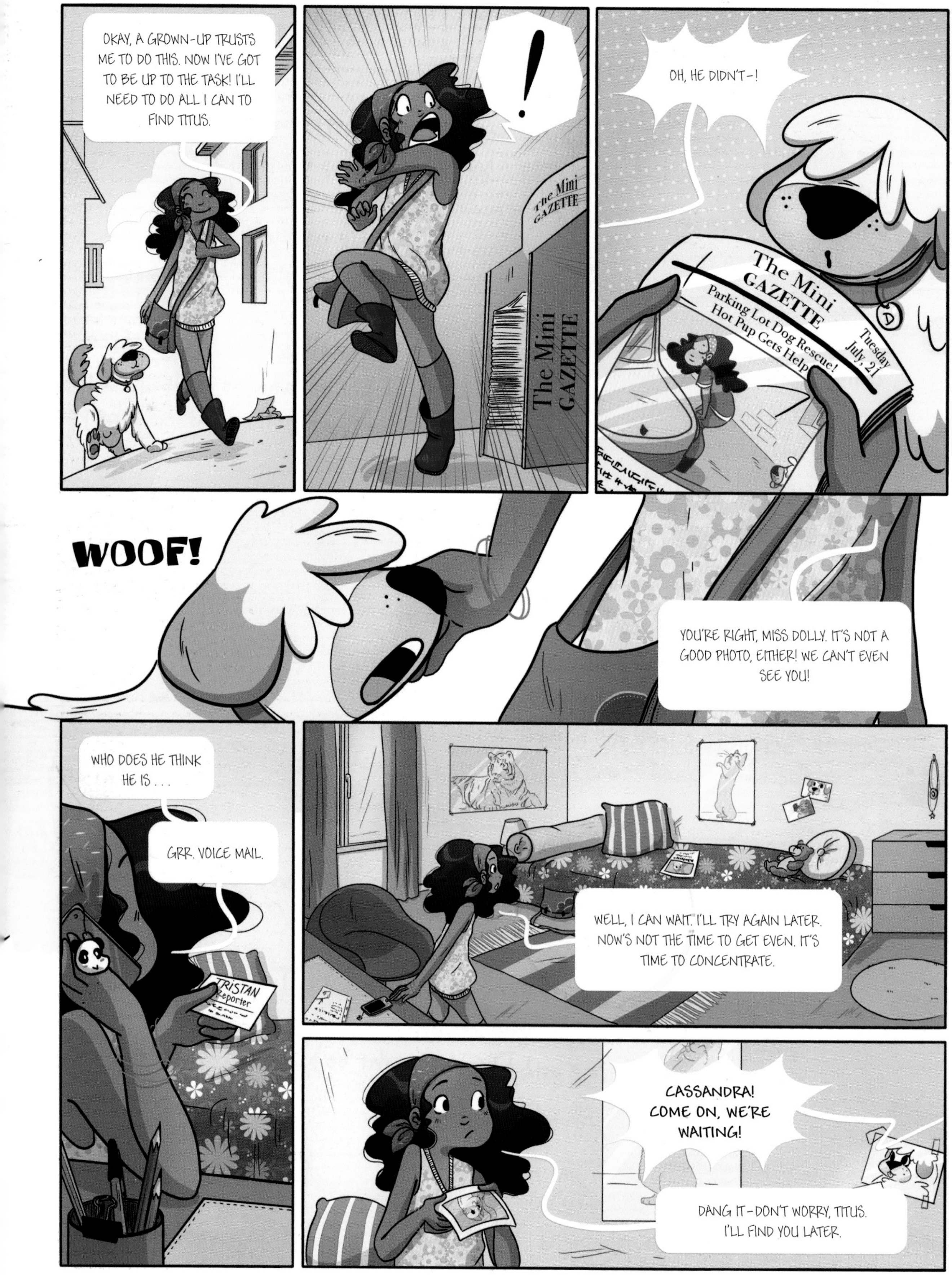

OKAY, A GROWN-UP TRUSTS ME TO DO THIS. NOW I'VE GOT TO BE UP TO THE TASK! I'LL NEED TO DO ALL I CAN TO FIND TITUS.
!
The Mini GAZETTE
The Mini GAZETTE
OH, HE DIDN'T-!
The Mini GAZETTE
Tuesday July, 21
Parking Lot Dog Rescue! Hot Pup Gets Help
WOOF!
YOU'RE RIGHT, MISS DOLLY. IT'S NOT A GOOD PHOTO, EITHER! WE CAN'T EVEN SEE YOU!
WHO DOES HE THINK HE IS . . .
GRR. VOICE MAIL.
TRISTAN Reporter
WELL, I CAN WAIT. I'LL TRY AGAIN LATER. NOW'S NOT THE TIME TO GET EVEN. IT'S TIME TO CONCENTRATE.
CASSANDRA! COME ON, WE'RE WAITING!
DANG IT-DON'T WORRY, TITUS. I'LL FIND YOU LATER.

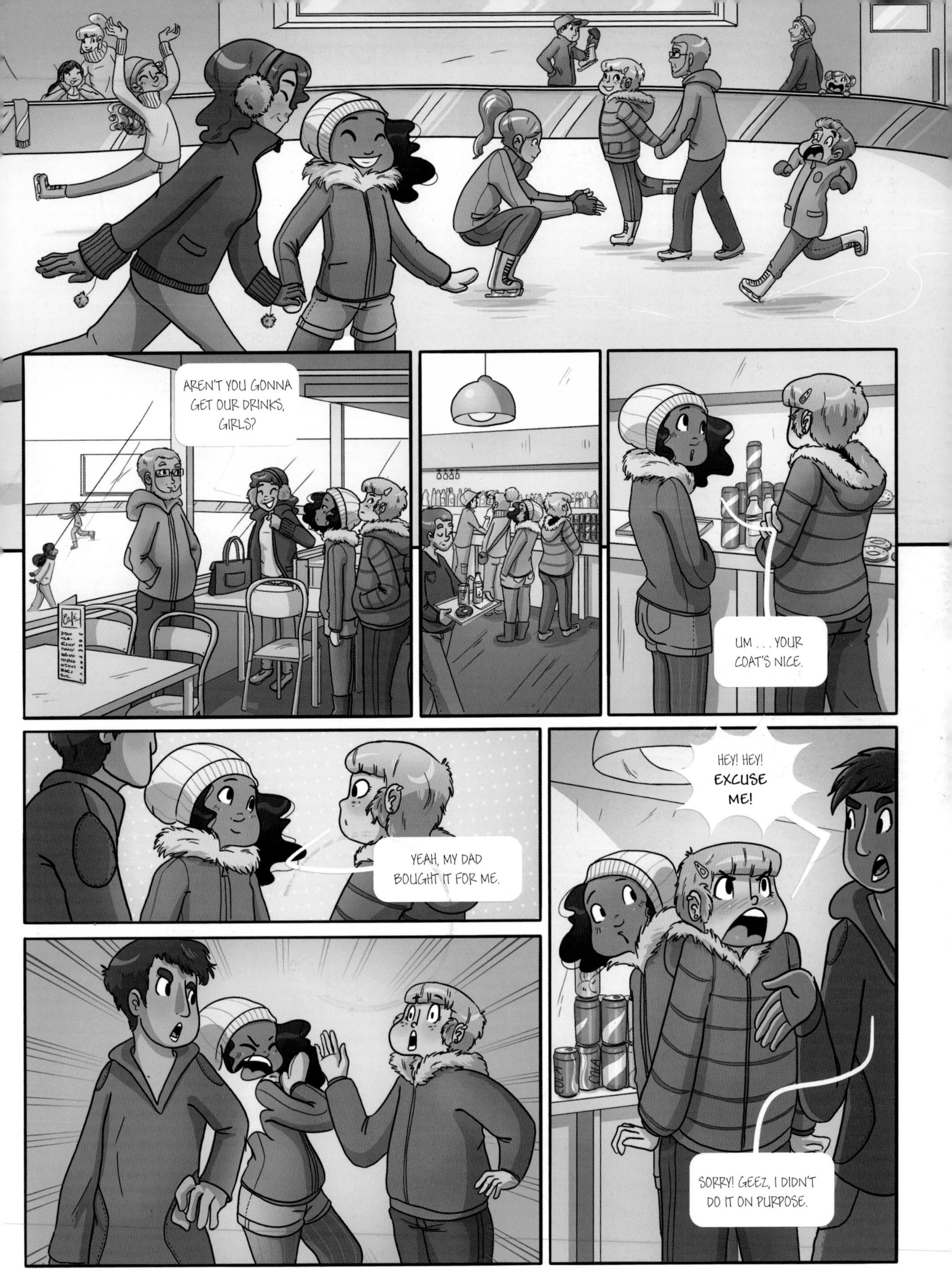
AREN'T YOU GONNA GET OUR DRINKS, GIRLS?
UM . . . YOUR COAT'S NICE.
YEAH, MY DAD BOUGHT IT FOR ME.
HEY! HEY! EXCUSE ME!
SORRY! GEEZ, I DIDN'T DO IT ON PURPOSE.

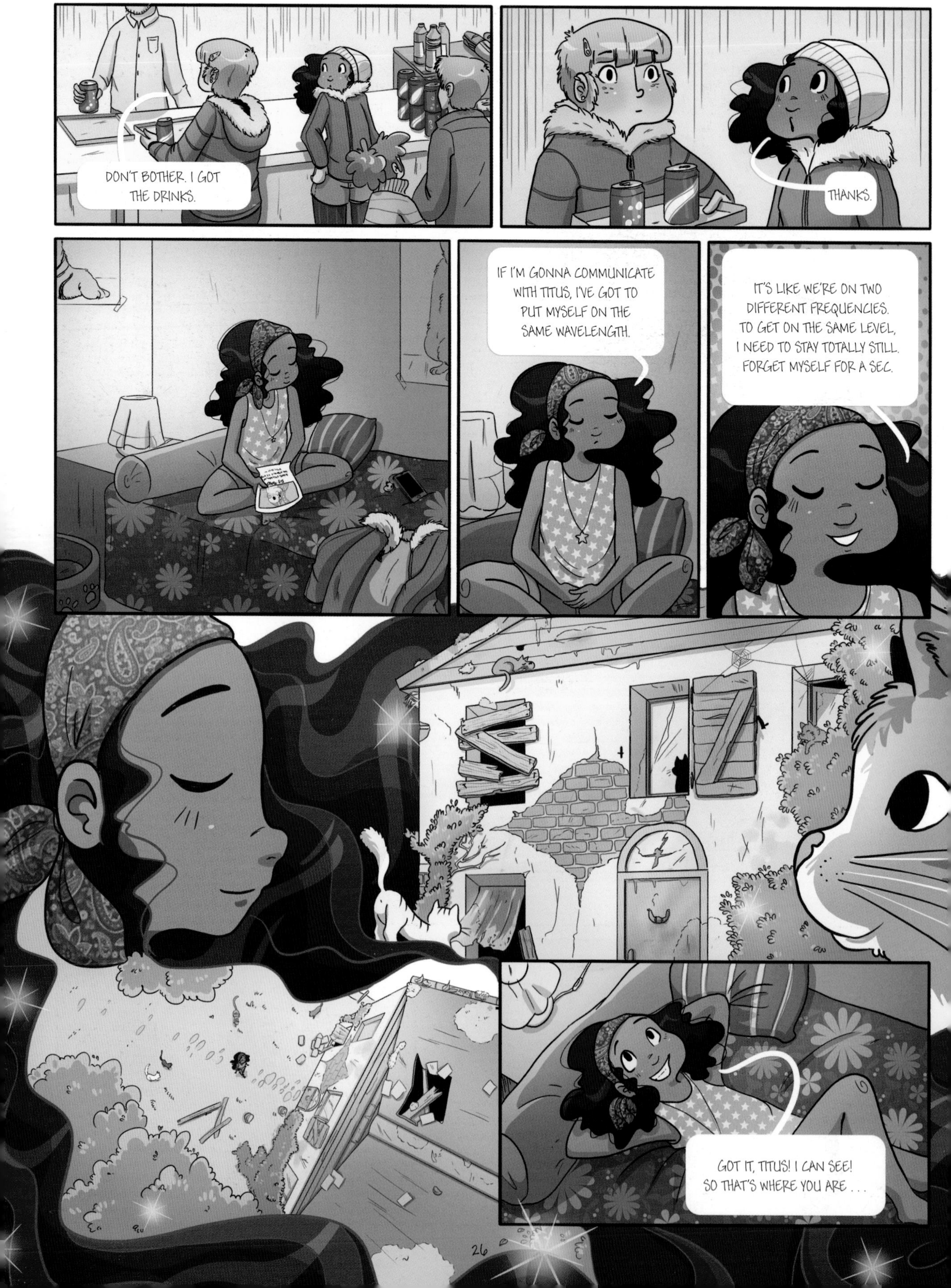

DON'T BOTHER. I GOT THE DRINKS.
THANKS.
IF I'M GONNA COMMUNICATE WITH TITUS, I'VE GOT TO PUT MYSELF ON THE SAME WAVELENGTH.
IT'S LIKE WE'RE ON TWO DIFFERENT FREQUENCIES. TO GET ON THE SAME LEVEL, I NEED TO STAY TOTALLY STILL. FORGET MYSELF FOR A SEC.
GOT IT, TITUS! I CAN SEE! SO THAT'S WHERE YOU ARE . . .

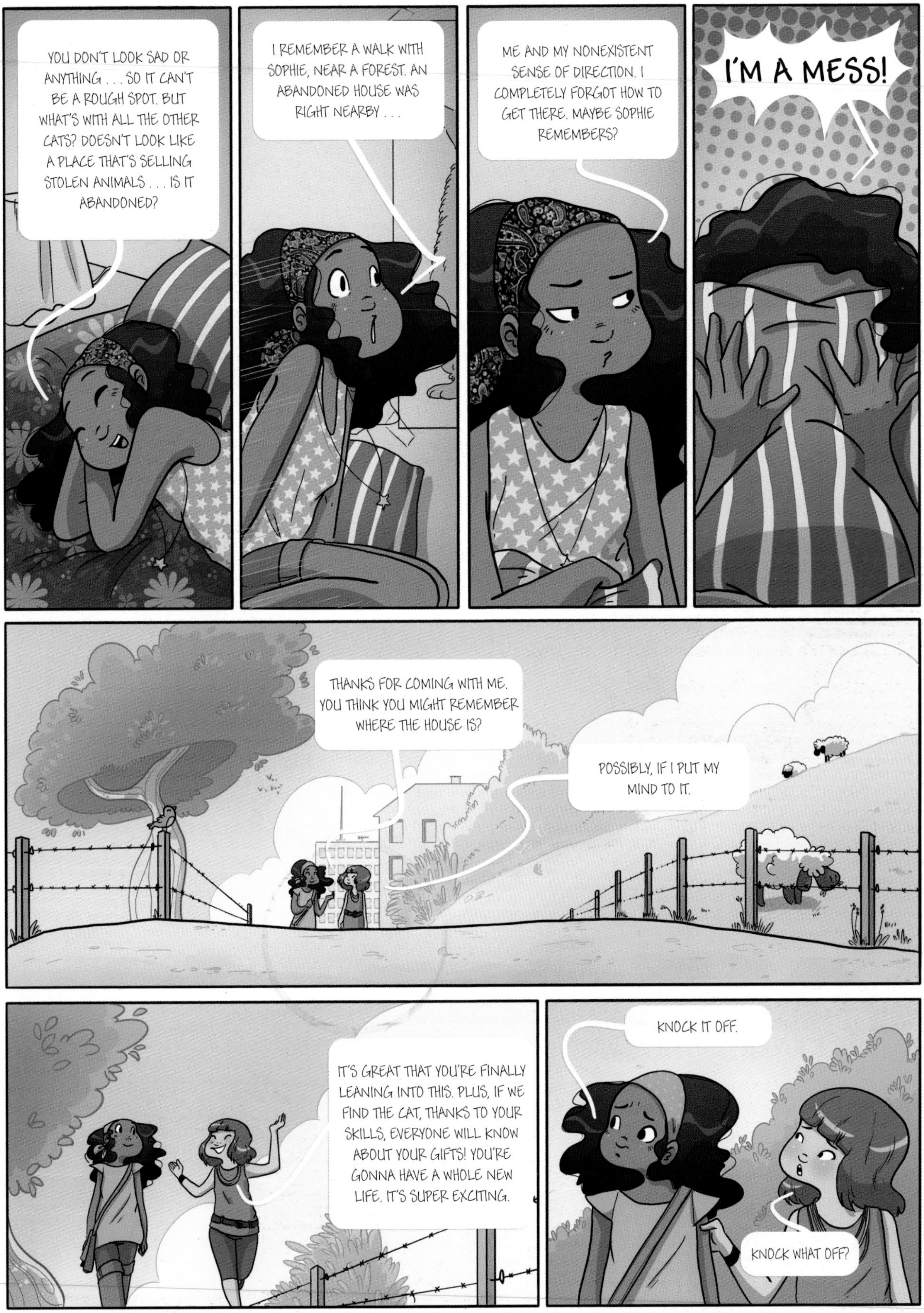
YOU DON'T LOOK SAD OR ANYTHING . . . SO IT CAN'T BE A ROUGH SPOT. BUT WHAT'S WITH ALL THE OTHER CATS? DOESN'T LOOK LIKE A PLACE THAT'S SELLING STOLEN ANIMALS . . . IS IT ABANDONED?
I REMEMBER A WALK WITH SOPHIE, NEAR A FOREST. AN ABANDONED HOUSE WAS RIGHT NEARBY . . .
ME AND MY NONEXISTENT SENSE OF DIRECTION. I COMPLETELY FORGOT HOW TO GET THERE. MAYBE SOPHIE REMEMBERS?
I'M A MESS!
THANKS FOR COMING WITH ME. YOU THINK YOU MIGHT REMEMBER WHERE THE HOUSE IS?
POSSIBLY, IF I PUT MY MIND TO IT.
IT'S GREAT THAT YOU'RE FINALLY LEANING INTO THIS. PLUS, IF WE FIND THE CAT, THANKS TO YOUR SKILLS, EVERYONE WILL KNOW ABOUT YOUR GIFTS! YOU'RE GONNA HAVE A WHOLE NEW LIFE. IT'S SUPER EXCITING.
KNOCK IT OFF.
KNOCK WHAT OFF?

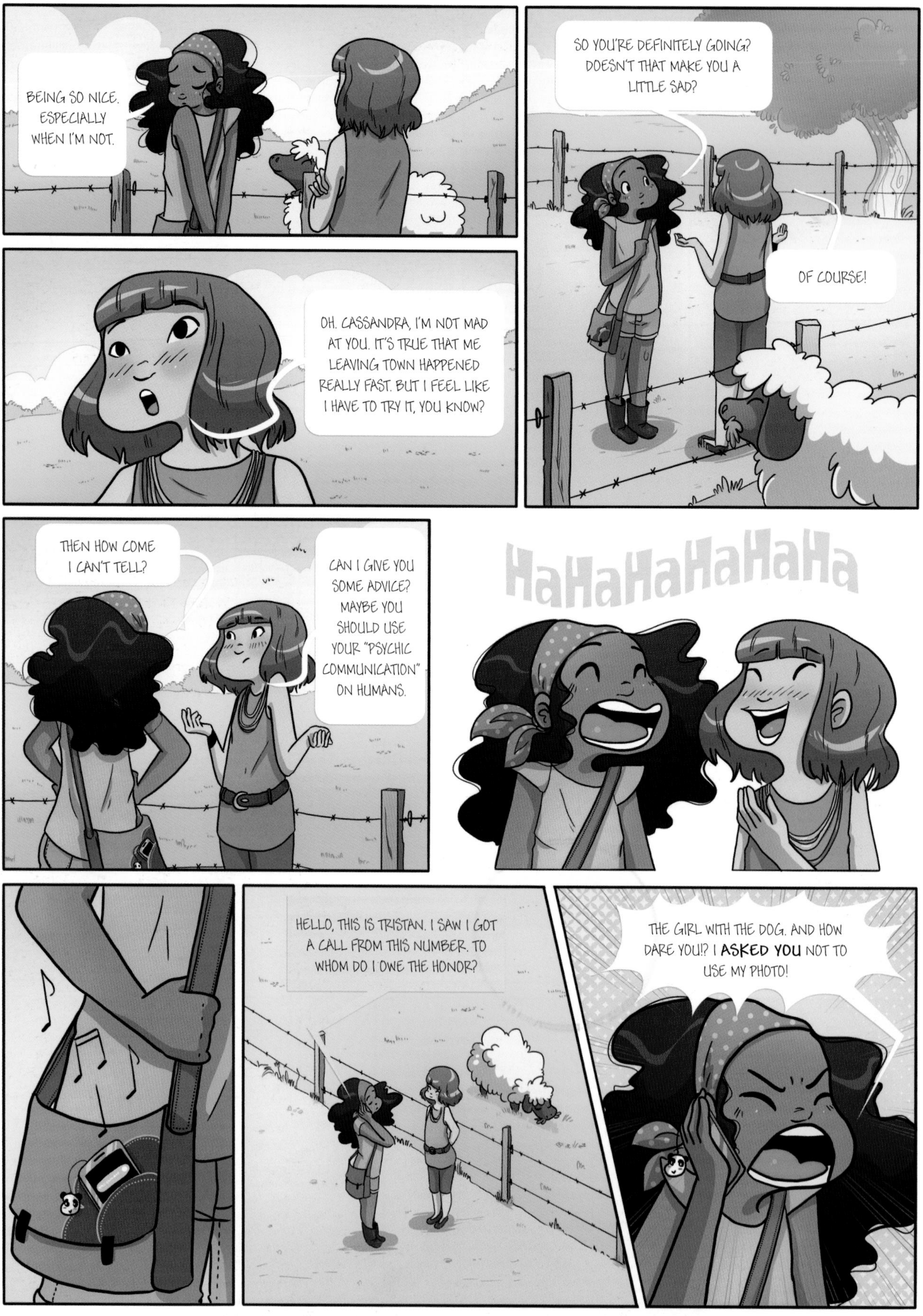
BEING SO NICE. ESPECIALLY WHEN I'M NOT.
SO YOU'RE DEFINITELY GOING? DOESN'T THAT MAKE YOU A LITTLE SAD?
OF COURSE!
OH. CASSANDRA, I'M NOT MAD AT YOU. IT'S TRUE THAT ME LEAVING TOWN HAPPENED REALLY FAST. BUT I FEEL LIKE I HAVE TO TRY IT, YOU KNOW?
THEN HOW COME I CAN'T TELL?
CAN I GIVE YOU SOME ADVICE? MAYBE YOU SHOULD USE YOUR "PSYCHIC COMMUNICATION" ON HUMANS.
HaHaHaHaHaHaHa
HELLO, THIS IS TRISTAN. I SAW I GOT A CALL FROM THIS NUMBER. TO WHOM DO I OWE THE HONOR?
THE GIRL WITH THE DOG. AND HOW DARE YOU!? I ASKED YOU NOT TO USE MY PHOTO!

I KNOW, I KNOW, I'M SORRY! BUT IT'S NOT OFTEN A STORY LIKE THAT COMES OUT OF NOWHERE. PLUS, MY ARTICLE'S ACTUALLY VERY NICE . . .

THAT IS NOT THE ISSUE!

BOO, YOU'RE NO FUN! HOW BOUT, SO THAT YOU'LL FORGIVE ME, I TAKE YOU TO A MOVIE?

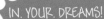

IN. YOUR. DREAMS!

WHO DOES HE THINK HE IS?

HERE WE ARE! I'M SURE THIS IS IT. I REMEMBER THE BARBED WIRE AT THE EDGES.

THE HOUSE IS . . . FLAT.

WELL, PEOPLE DON'T ALWAYS SUCCEED THE FIRST TIME. YOU'RE GONNA GET THERE, CASSANDRA.

AH, THERE'S NO FIGHTING IT! YOU CAN'T STOP BEING NICE.

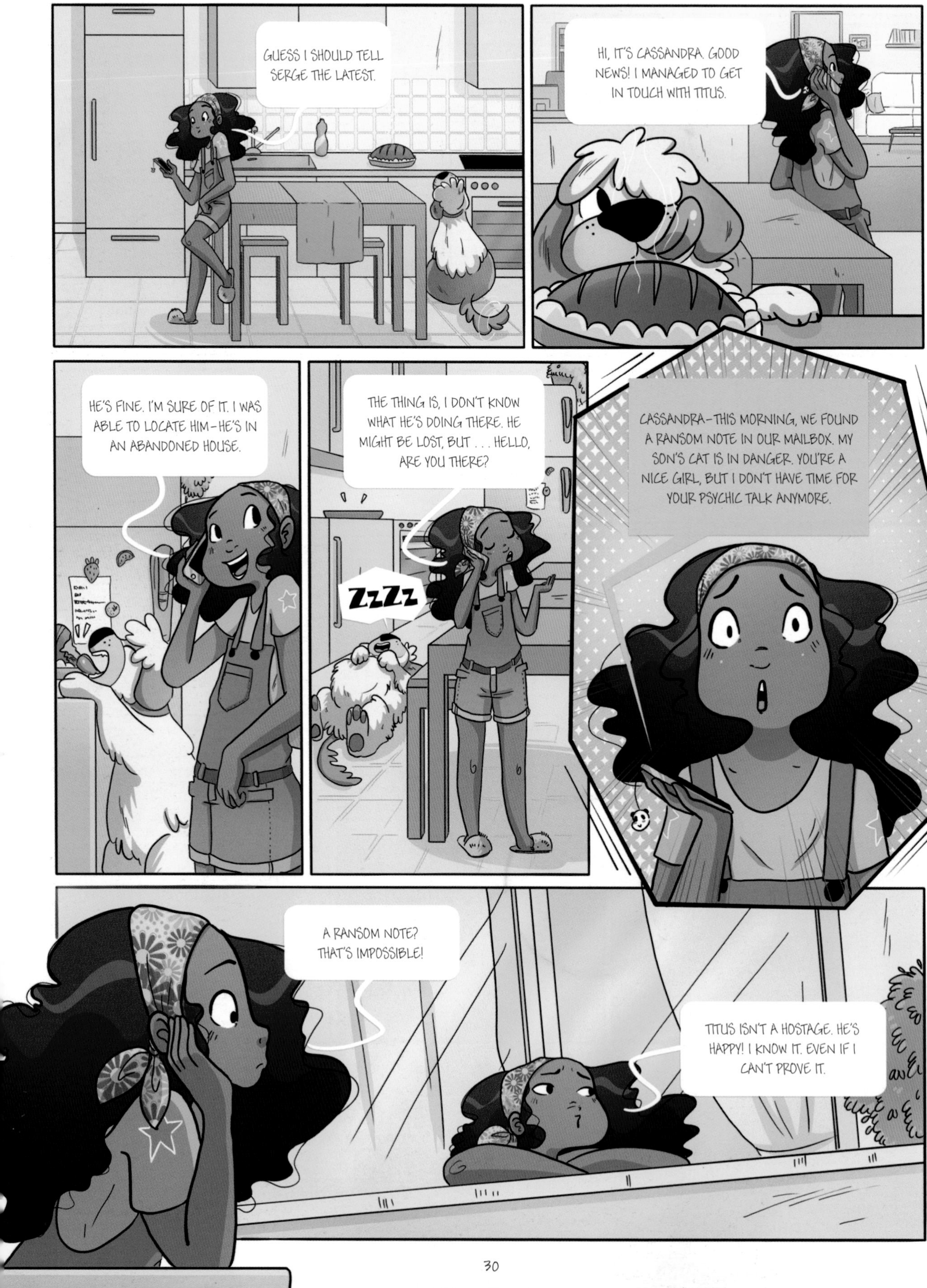
GUESS I SHOULD TELL SERGE THE LATEST.
HI, IT'S CASSANDRA. GOOD NEWS! I MANAGED TO GET IN TOUCH WITH TITUS.
HE'S FINE. I'M SURE OF IT. I WAS ABLE TO LOCATE HIM—HE'S IN AN ABANDONED HOUSE.
THE THING IS, I DON'T KNOW WHAT HE'S DOING THERE. HE MIGHT BE LOST, BUT . . . HELLO, ARE YOU THERE?
ZZZZ
CASSANDRA—THIS MORNING, WE FOUND A RANSOM NOTE IN OUR MAILBOX. MY SON'S CAT IS IN DANGER. YOU'RE A NICE GIRL, BUT I DON'T HAVE TIME FOR YOUR PSYCHIC TALK ANYMORE.
A RANSOM NOTE? THAT'S IMPOSSIBLE!
TITUS ISN'T A HOSTAGE. HE'S HAPPY! I KNOW IT. EVEN IF I CAN'T PROVE IT.

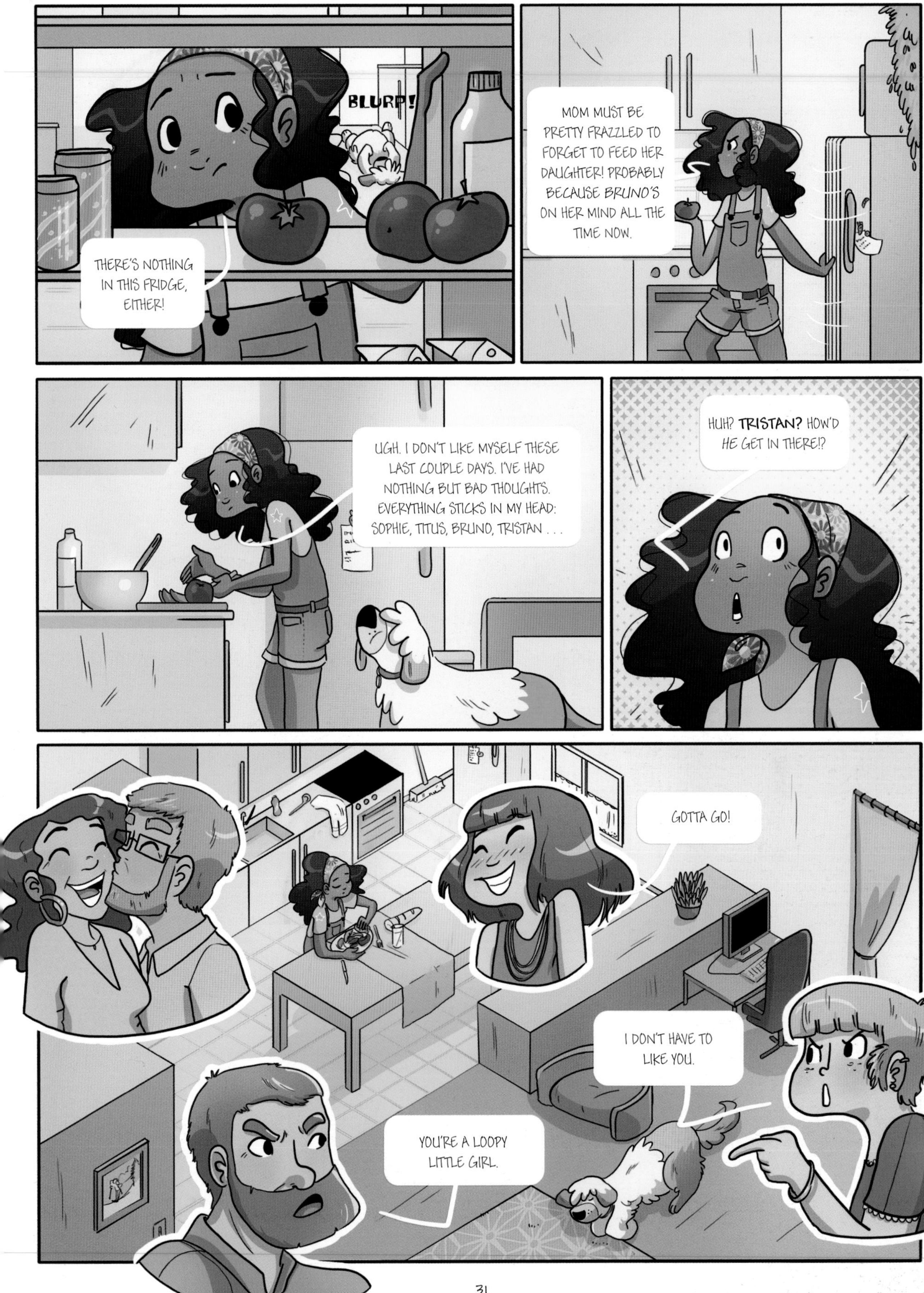
BLURP!
THERE'S NOTHING IN THIS FRIDGE, EITHER!
MOM MUST BE PRETTY FRAZZLED TO FORGET TO FEED HER DAUGHTER! PROBABLY BECAUSE BRUNO'S ON HER MIND ALL THE TIME NOW.
UGH. I DON'T LIKE MYSELF THESE LAST COUPLE DAYS. I'VE HAD NOTHING BUT BAD THOUGHTS. EVERYTHING STICKS IN MY HEAD: SOPHIE, TITUS, BRUNO, TRISTAN . . .
HUH? **TRISTAN?** HOW'D HE GET IN THERE!?
GOTTA GO!
I DON'T HAVE TO LIKE YOU.
YOU'RE A LOOPY LITTLE GIRL.

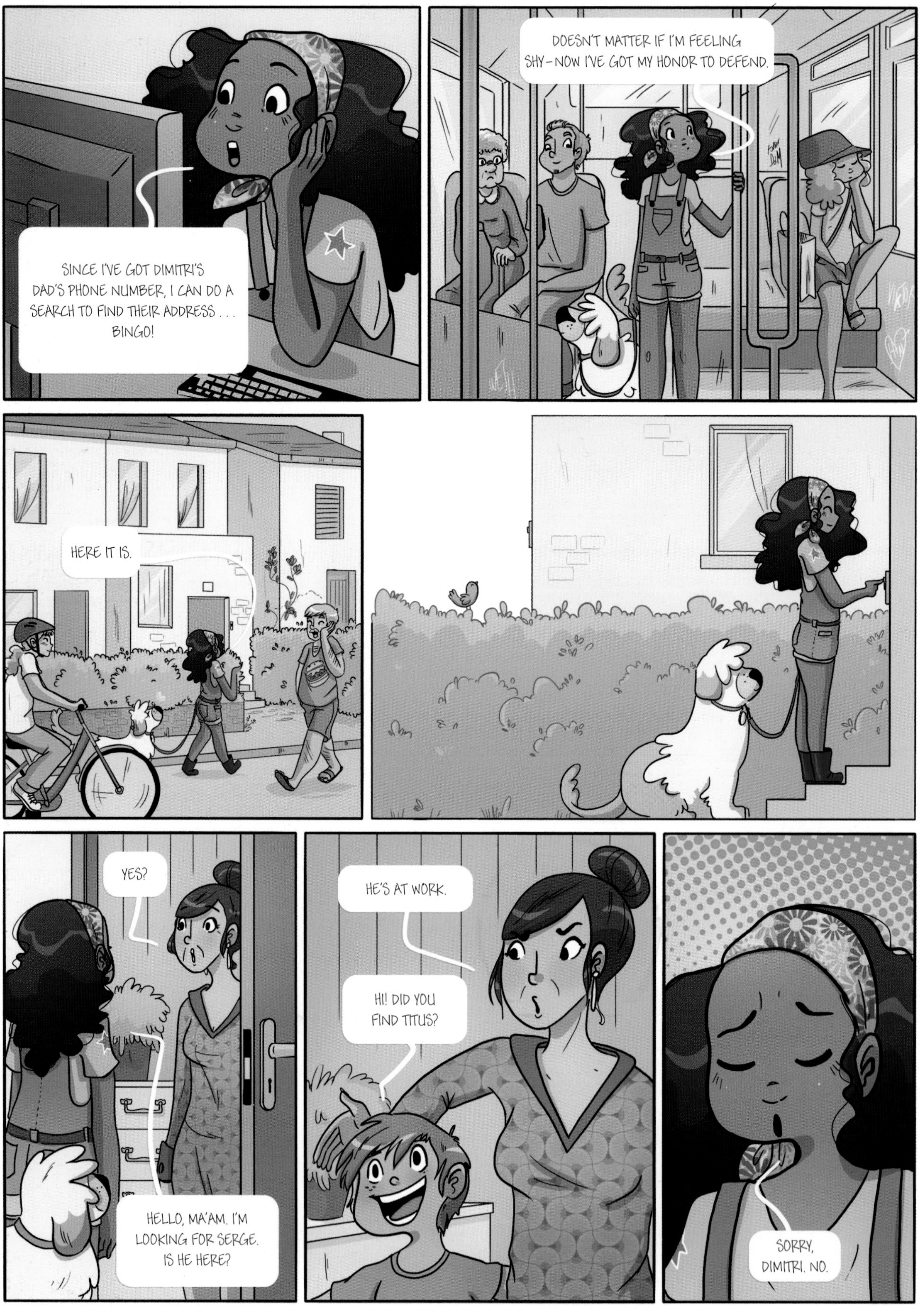
SINCE I'VE GOT DIMITRI'S DAD'S PHONE NUMBER, I CAN DO A SEARCH TO FIND THEIR ADDRESS . . . BINGO!
DOESN'T MATTER IF I'M FEELING SHY—NOW I'VE GOT MY HONOR TO DEFEND.
HERE IT IS.
YES?
HELLO, MA'AM. I'M LOOKING FOR SERGE. IS HE HERE?
HE'S AT WORK.
HI! DID YOU FIND TITUS?
SORRY, DIMITRI. NO.

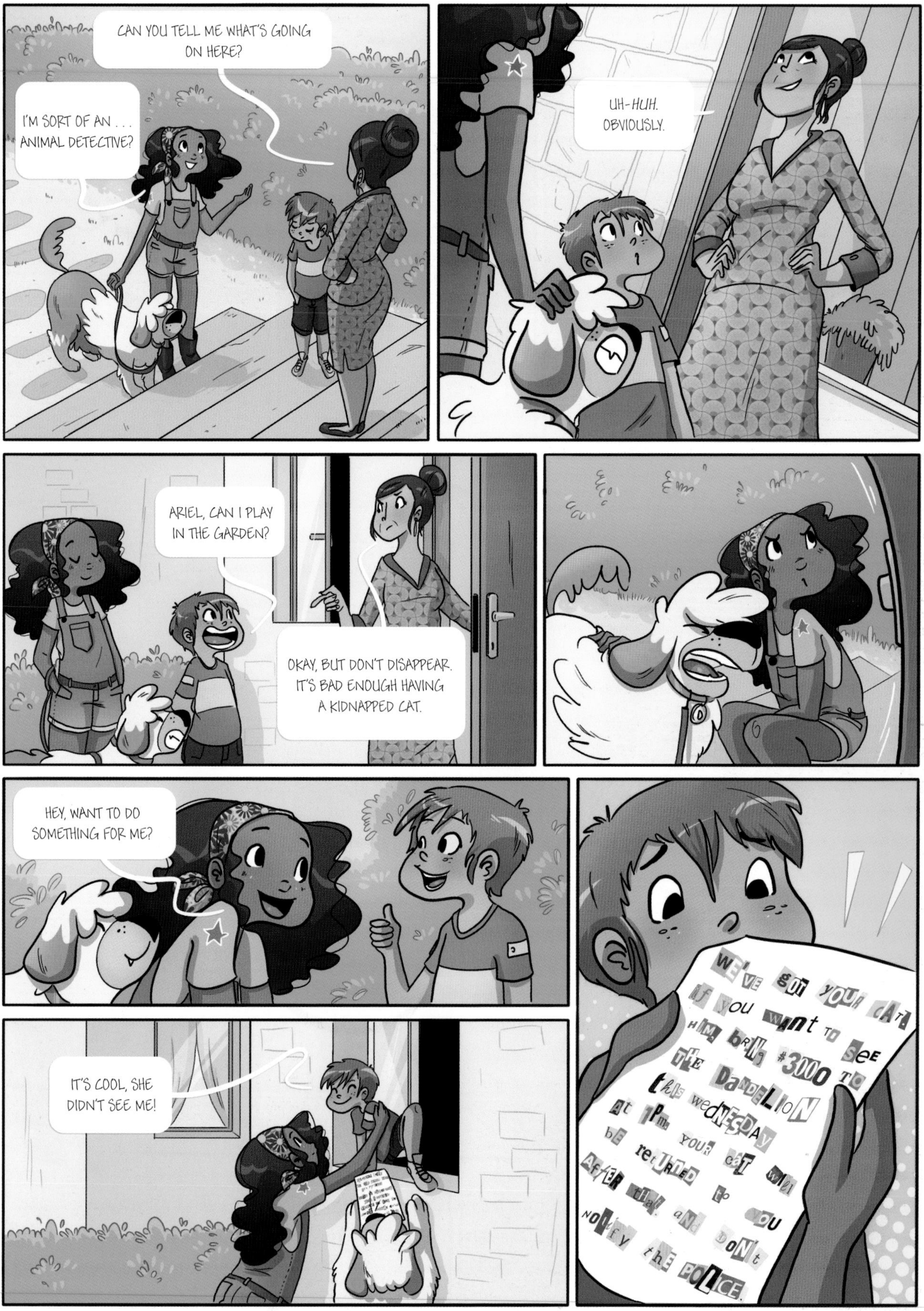
CAN YOU TELL ME WHAT'S GOING ON HERE?
I'M SORT OF AN . . . ANIMAL DETECTIVE?
UH-HUH. OBVIOUSLY.
ARIEL, CAN I PLAY IN THE GARDEN?
OKAY, BUT DON'T DISAPPEAR. IT'S BAD ENOUGH HAVING A KIDNAPPED CAT.
HEY, WANT TO DO SOMETHING FOR ME?
IT'S COOL, SHE DIDN'T SEE ME!
WE'VE GOT YOUR CAT IF YOU WANT TO SEE HIM BRING #3000 TO THE DANDELION THIS WEDNESDAY AT 1PM. YOUR CAT WILL BE RETURNED TO YOU AFTER THAT. AND DON'T NOTIFY THE POLICE.

WE FOUND IT IN THE MAILBOX. NO ENVELOPE.

WHAT ARE YOU DOING HERE? I THOUGHT I WAS CLEAR ABOUT . . .

LISTEN—TITUS HAS NOT BEEN KIDNAPPED. I KNOW IT!

BLLLLLUUUUURRRRUGGGG!

THAT DOESN'T LOOK LIKE KIBBLE . . . I DON'T BELIEVE IT! YOU STOLE MY BREAKFAST! THAT'S WHAT YOU GET, MISS DOLLY!

SORRY ABOUT THAT. I'LL CLEAN IT UP.

THAT'S ALL RIGHT. I'D RATHER YOU LEAVE. AND NOT SET FOOT HERE AGAIN.

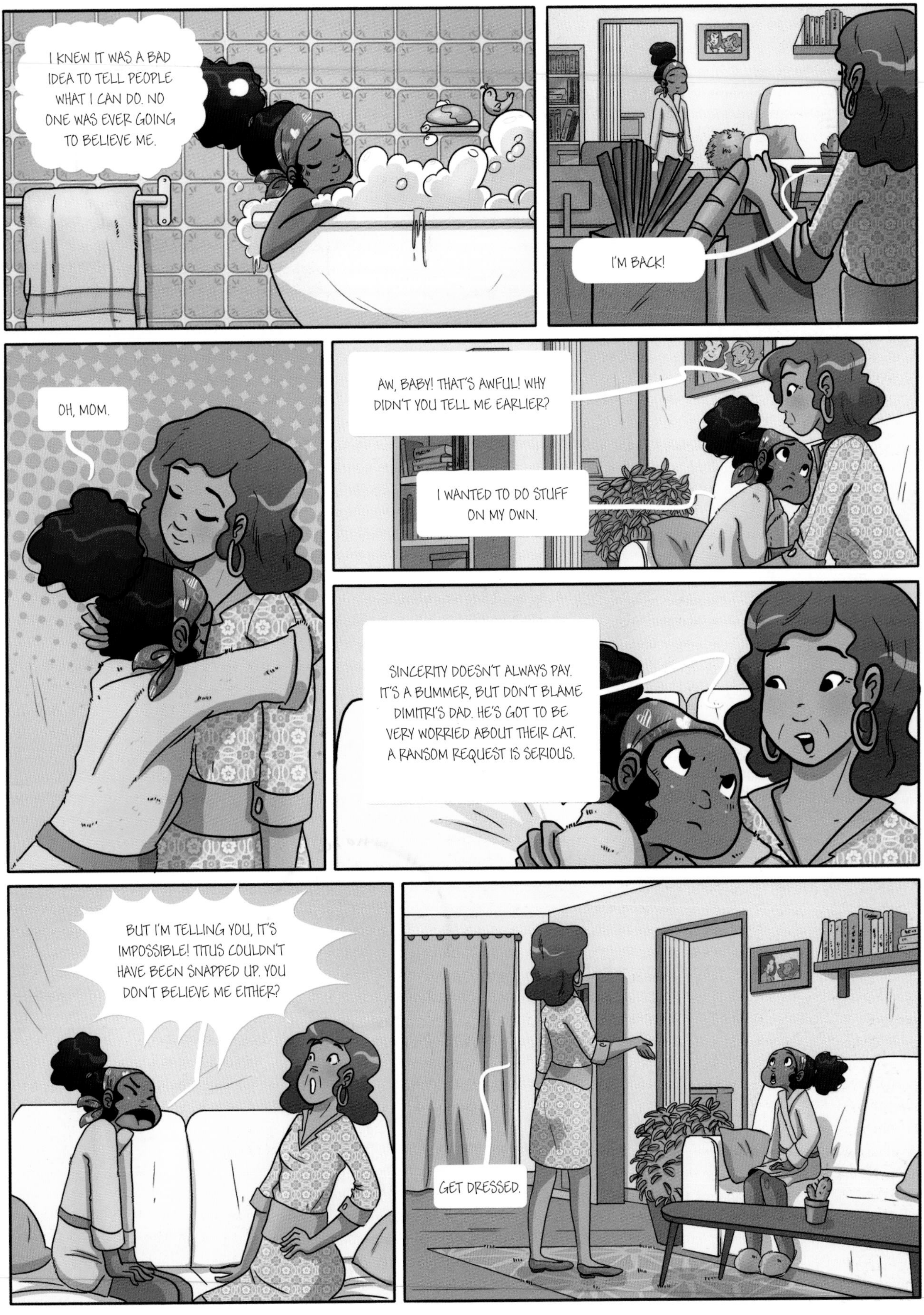
I KNEW IT WAS A BAD IDEA TO TELL PEOPLE WHAT I CAN DO. NO ONE WAS EVER GOING TO BELIEVE ME.
I'M BACK!
OH, MOM.
AW, BABY! THAT'S AWFUL! WHY DIDN'T YOU TELL ME EARLIER?
I WANTED TO DO STUFF ON MY OWN.
SINCERITY DOESN'T ALWAYS PAY. IT'S A BUMMER, BUT DON'T BLAME DIMITRI'S DAD. HE'S GOT TO BE VERY WORRIED ABOUT THEIR CAT. A RANSOM REQUEST IS SERIOUS.
BUT I'M TELLING YOU, IT'S IMPOSSIBLE! TITUS COULDN'T HAVE BEEN SNAPPED UP. YOU DON'T BELIEVE ME EITHER?
GET DRESSED.

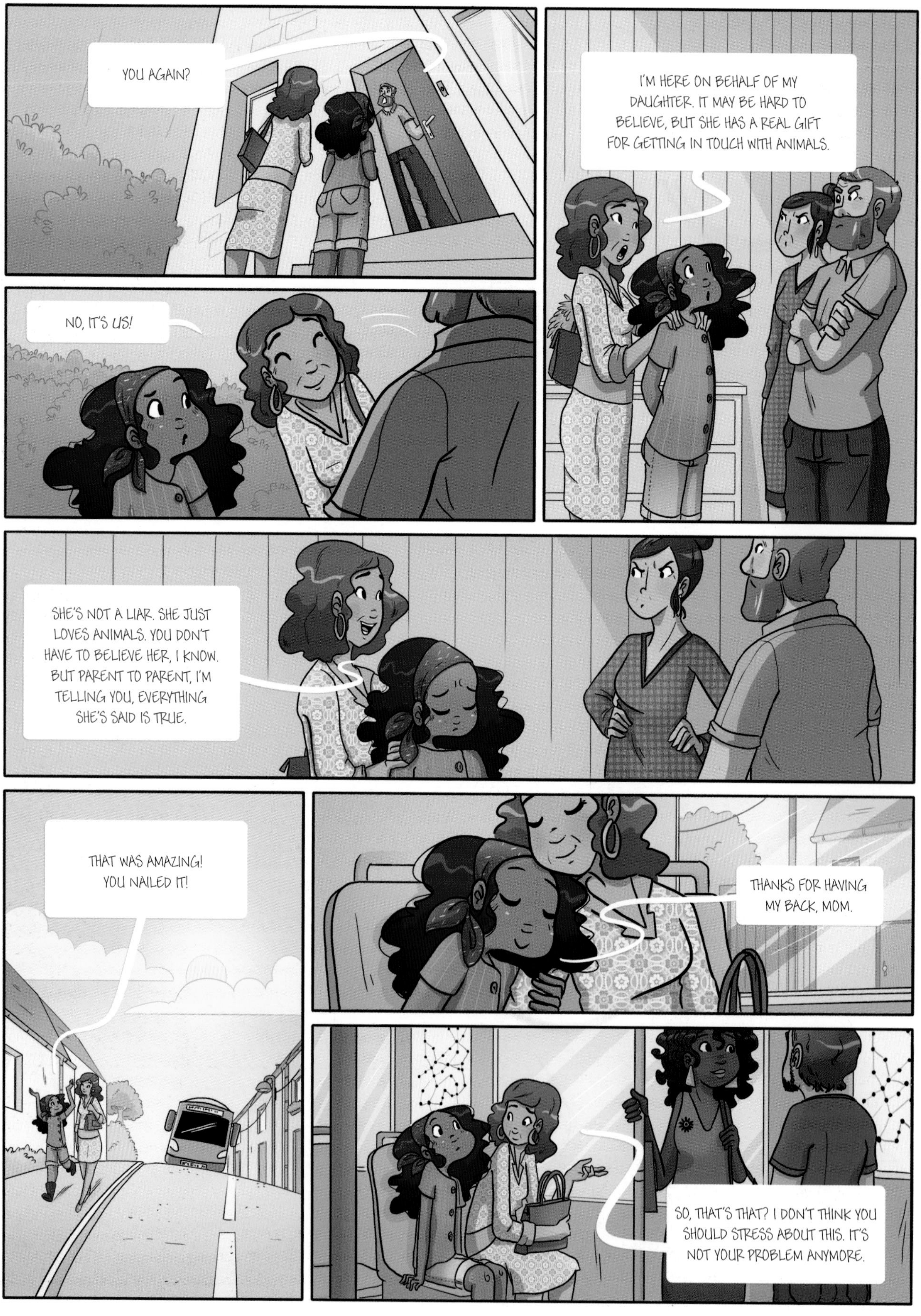
YOU AGAIN?
I'M HERE ON BEHALF OF MY DAUGHTER. IT MAY BE HARD TO BELIEVE, BUT SHE HAS A REAL GIFT FOR GETTING IN TOUCH WITH ANIMALS.
NO, IT'S US!
SHE'S NOT A LIAR. SHE JUST LOVES ANIMALS. YOU DON'T HAVE TO BELIEVE HER, I KNOW. BUT PARENT TO PARENT, I'M TELLING YOU, EVERYTHING SHE'S SAID IS TRUE.
THAT WAS AMAZING! YOU NAILED IT!
THANKS FOR HAVING MY BACK, MOM.
SO, THAT'S THAT? I DON'T THINK YOU SHOULD STRESS ABOUT THIS. IT'S NOT YOUR PROBLEM ANYMORE.

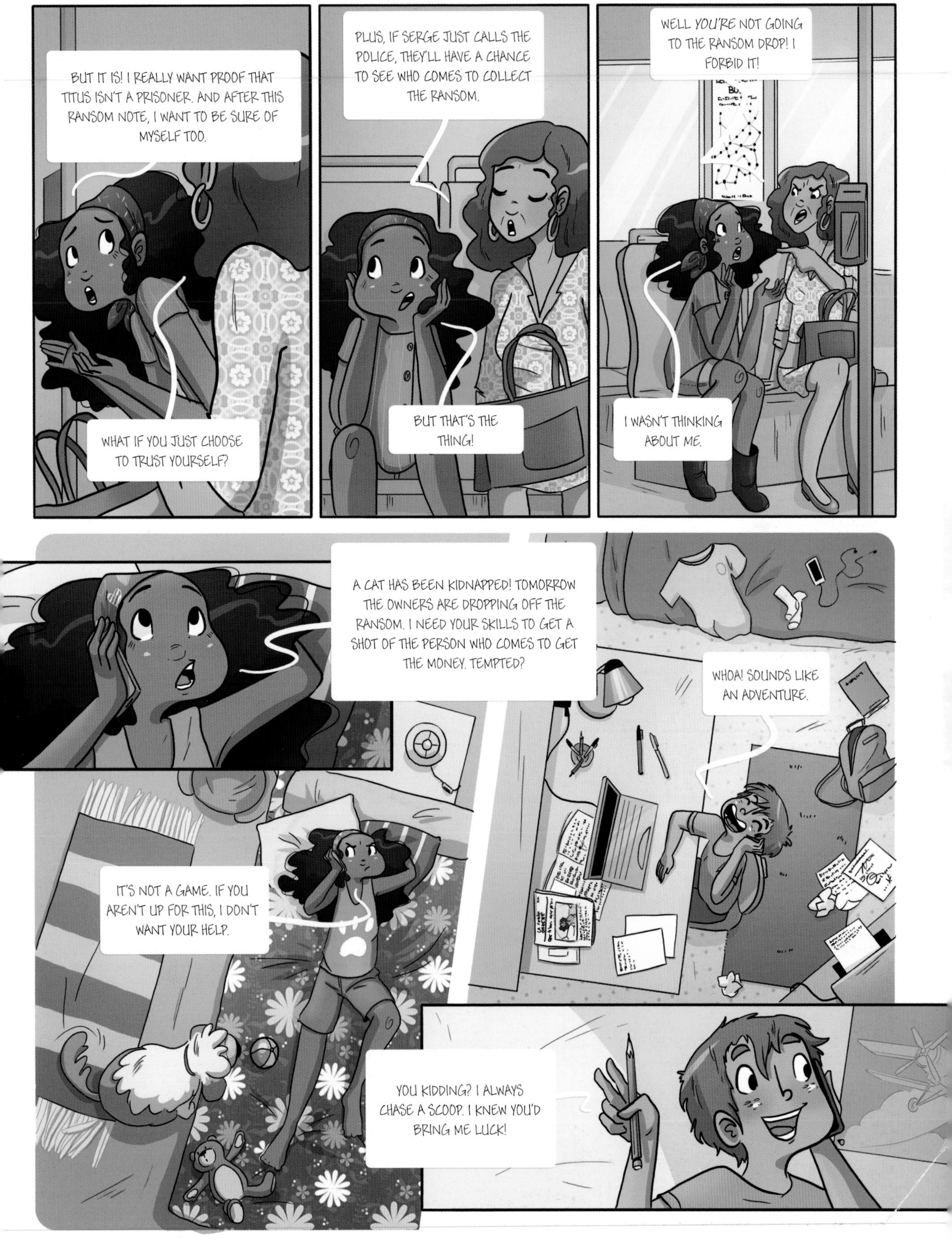
BUT IT IS! I REALLY WANT PROOF THAT TITUS ISN'T A PRISONER. AND AFTER THIS RANSOM NOTE, I WANT TO BE SURE OF MYSELF TOO.
WHAT IF YOU JUST CHOOSE TO TRUST YOURSELF?
PLUS, IF SERGE JUST CALLS THE POLICE, THEY'LL HAVE A CHANCE TO SEE WHO COMES TO COLLECT THE RANSOM.
BUT THAT'S THE THING!
WELL YOU'RE NOT GOING TO THE RANSOM DROP! I FORBID IT!
I WASN'T THINKING ABOUT ME.
A CAT HAS BEEN KIDNAPPED! TOMORROW THE OWNERS ARE DROPPING OFF THE RANSOM. I NEED YOUR SKILLS TO GET A SHOT OF THE PERSON WHO COMES TO GET THE MONEY. TEMPTED?
WHOA! SOUNDS LIKE AN ADVENTURE.
IT'S NOT A GAME. IF YOU AREN'T UP FOR THIS, I DON'T WANT YOUR HELP.
YOU KIDDING? I ALWAYS CHASE A SCOOP. I KNEW YOU'D BRING ME LUCK!

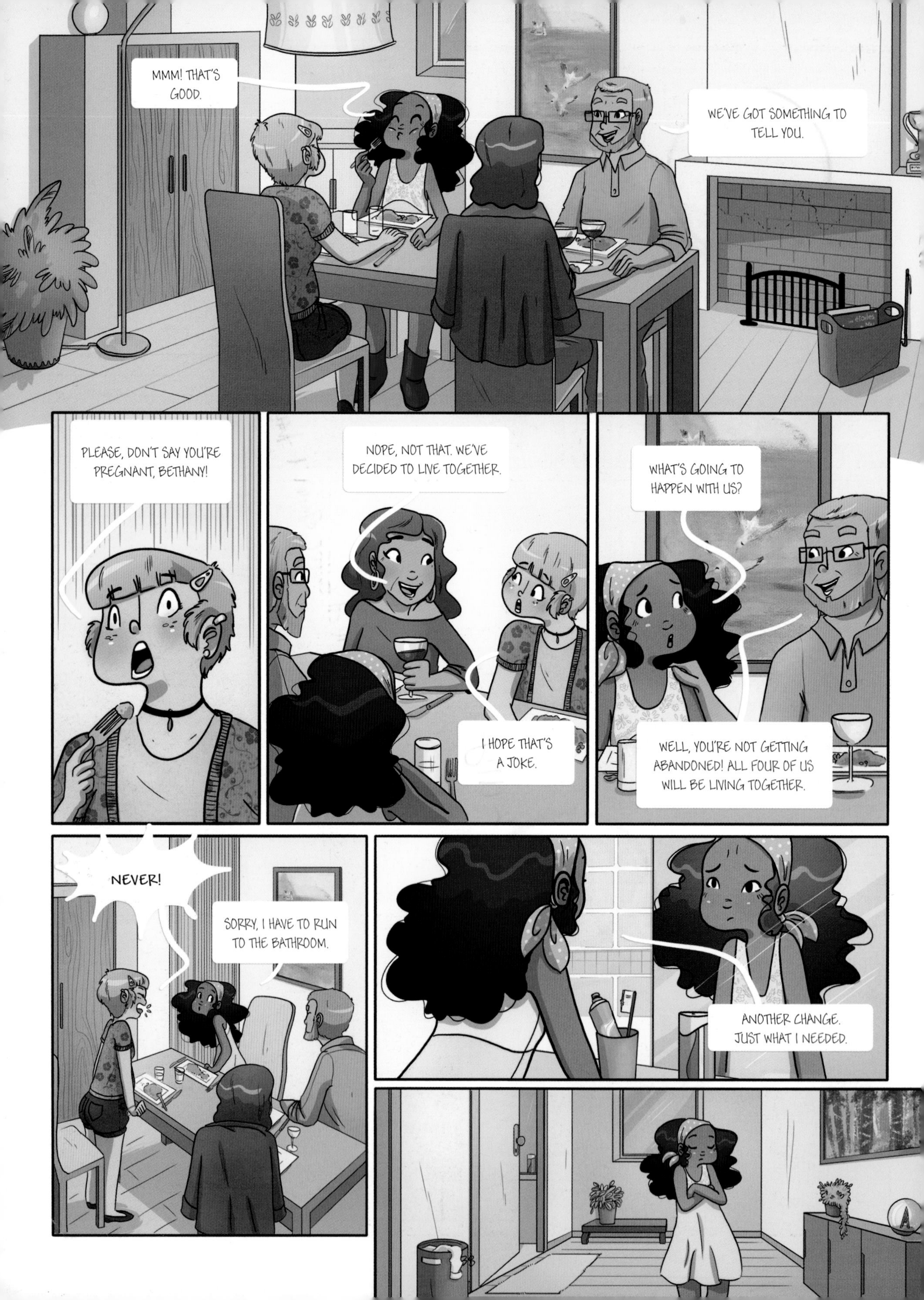
MMM! THAT'S GOOD.
WE'VE GOT SOMETHING TO TELL YOU.
PLEASE, DON'T SAY YOU'RE PREGNANT, BETHANY!
NOPE, NOT THAT. WE'VE DECIDED TO LIVE TOGETHER.
I HOPE THAT'S A JOKE.
WHAT'S GOING TO HAPPEN WITH US?
WELL, YOU'RE NOT GETTING ABANDONED! ALL FOUR OF US WILL BE LIVING TOGETHER.
NEVER!
SORRY, I HAVE TO RUN TO THE BATHROOM.
ANOTHER CHANGE. JUST WHAT I NEEDED.

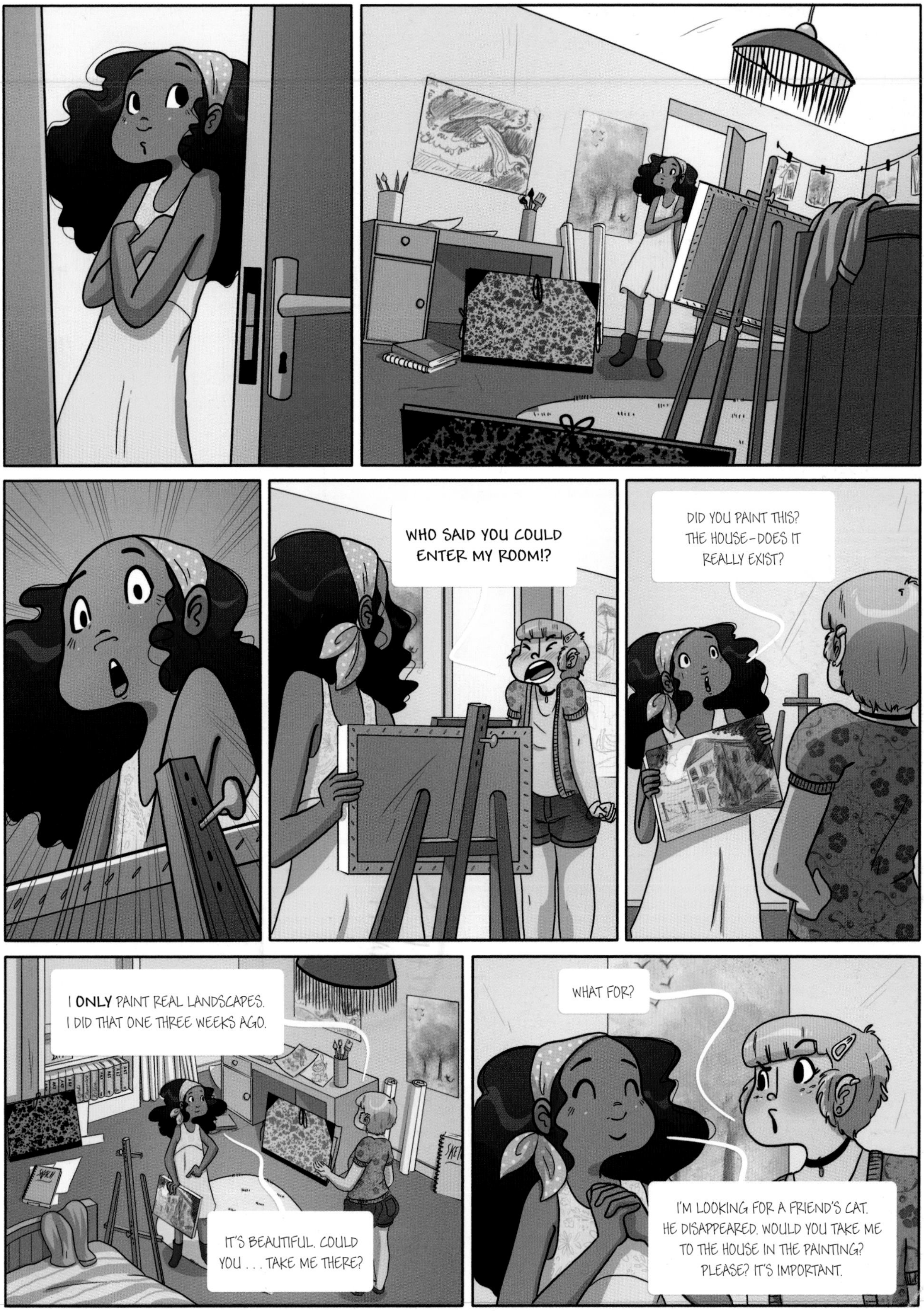
WHO SAID YOU COULD ENTER MY ROOM!?
DID YOU PAINT THIS? THE HOUSE—DOES IT REALLY EXIST?
I **ONLY** PAINT REAL LANDSCAPES. I DID THAT ONE THREE WEEKS AGO.
IT'S BEAUTIFUL. COULD YOU . . . TAKE ME THERE?
WHAT FOR?
I'M LOOKING FOR A FRIEND'S CAT. HE DISAPPEARED. WOULD YOU TAKE ME TO THE HOUSE IN THE PAINTING? PLEASE? IT'S IMPORTANT.

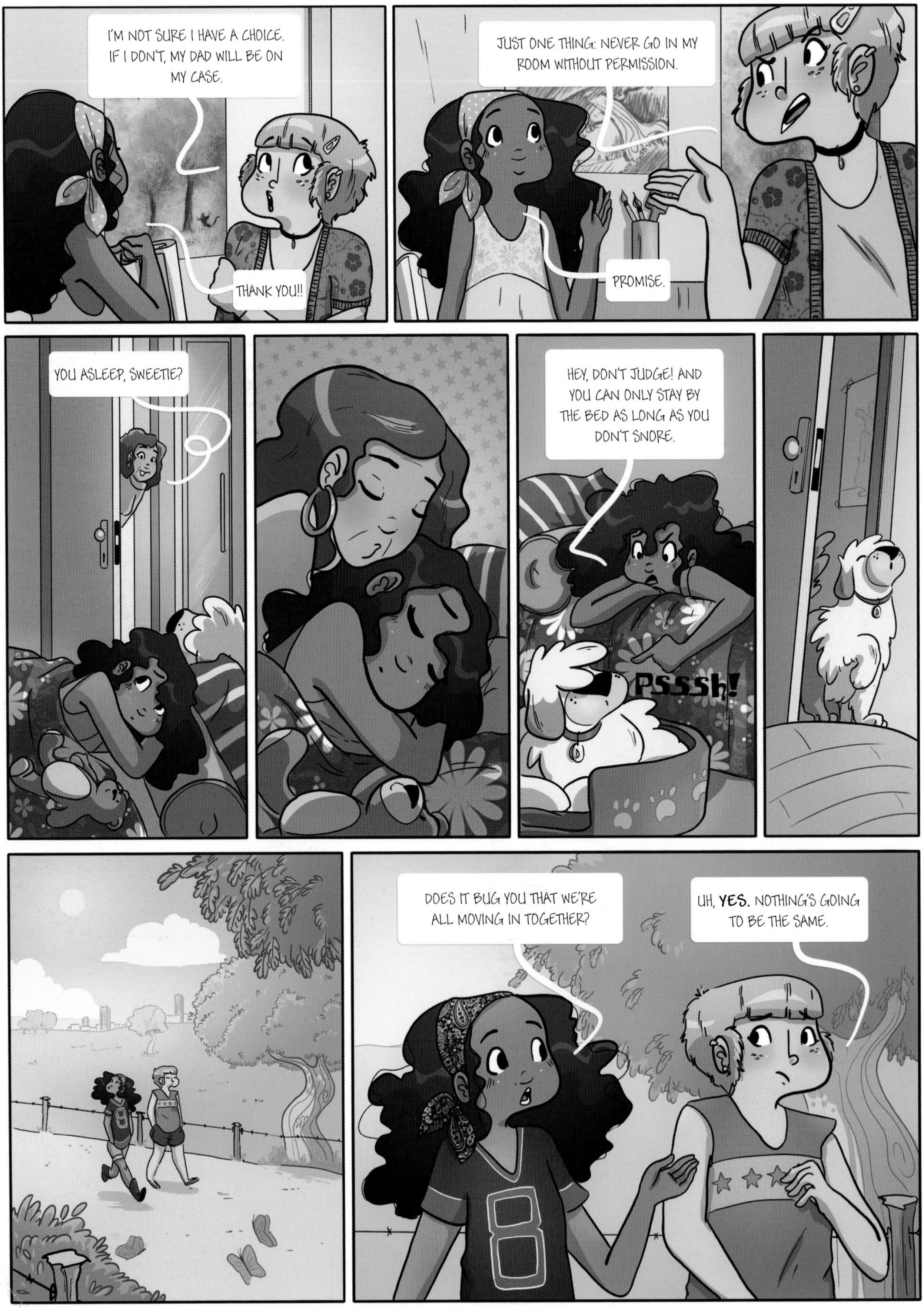
I'M NOT SURE I HAVE A CHOICE. IF I DON'T, MY DAD WILL BE ON MY CASE.
THANK YOU!!
JUST ONE THING: NEVER GO IN MY ROOM WITHOUT PERMISSION.
PROMISE.
YOU ASLEEP, SWEETIE?
HEY, DON'T JUDGE! AND YOU CAN ONLY STAY BY THE BED AS LONG AS YOU DON'T SNORE.
PSSSh!
DOES IT BUG YOU THAT WE'RE ALL MOVING IN TOGETHER?
UH, **YES.** NOTHING'S GOING TO BE THE SAME.

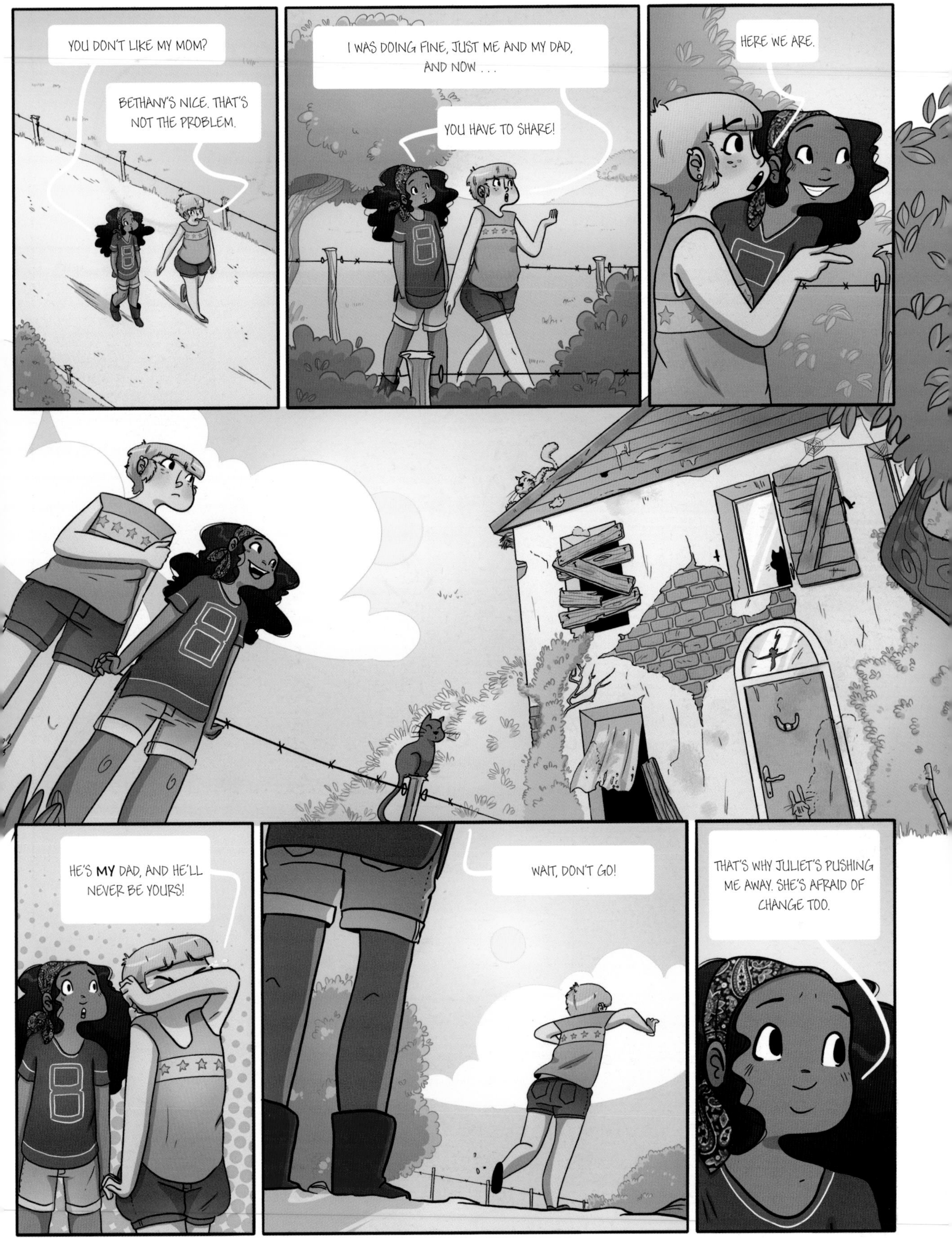
YOU DON'T LIKE MY MOM?
BETHANY'S NICE. THAT'S NOT THE PROBLEM.
I WAS DOING FINE, JUST ME AND MY DAD, AND NOW . . .
YOU HAVE TO SHARE!
HERE WE ARE.
HE'S **MY** DAD, AND HE'LL NEVER BE YOURS!
WAIT, DON'T GO!
THAT'S WHY JULIET'S PUSHING ME AWAY. SHE'S AFRAID OF CHANGE TOO.

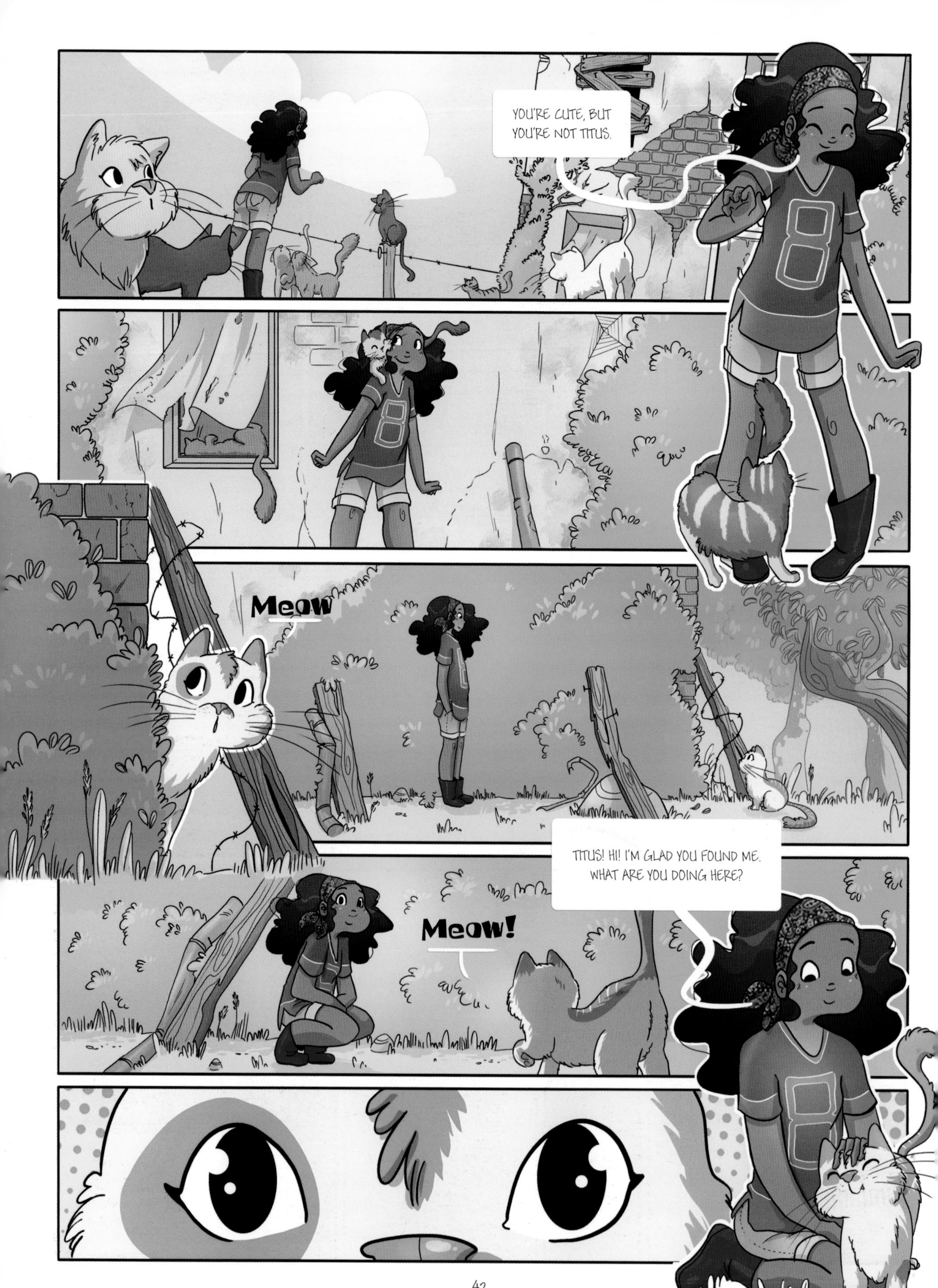
YOU'RE CUTE, BUT YOU'RE NOT TITUS.
Meow
Meow!
TITUS! HI! I'M GLAD YOU FOUND ME. WHAT ARE YOU DOING HERE?

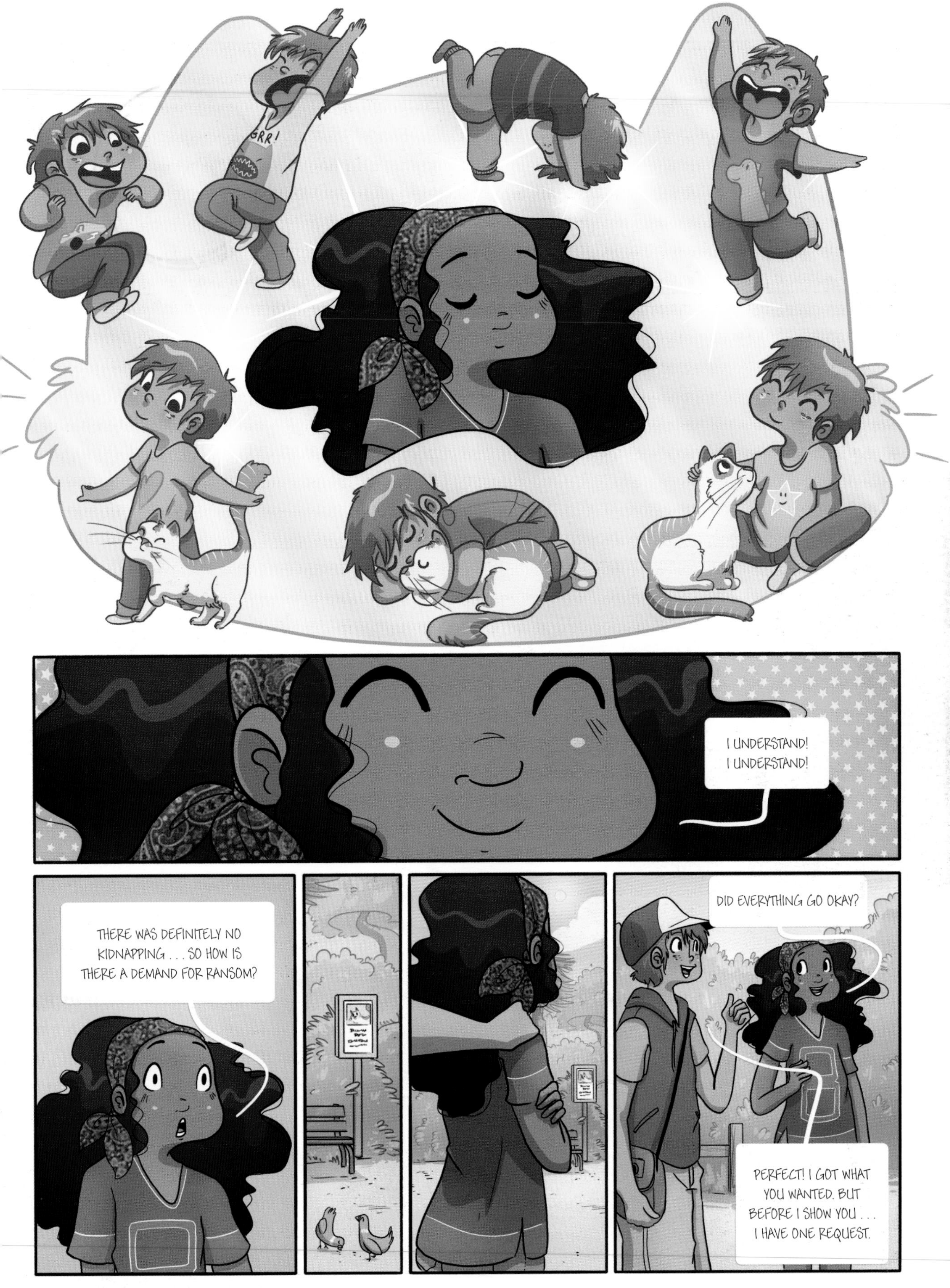
GRR!
I UNDERSTAND!
I UNDERSTAND!
THERE WAS DEFINITELY NO KIDNAPPING . . . SO HOW IS THERE A DEMAND FOR RANSOM?
DID EVERYTHING GO OKAY?
PERFECT! I GOT WHAT YOU WANTED. BUT BEFORE I SHOW YOU . . . I HAVE ONE REQUEST.

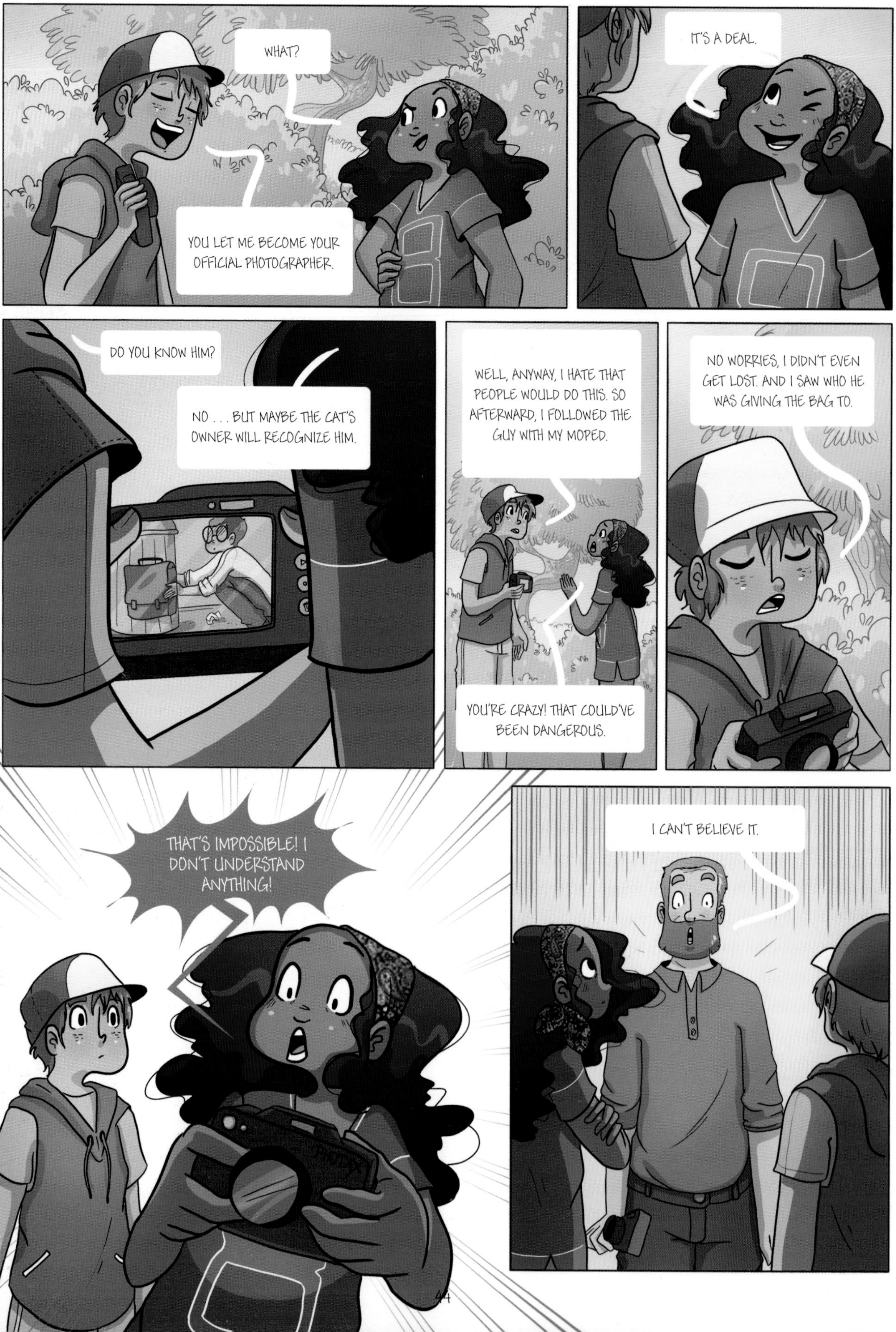
WHAT?
YOU LET ME BECOME YOUR OFFICIAL PHOTOGRAPHER.
IT'S A DEAL.
DO YOU KNOW HIM?
NO . . . BUT MAYBE THE CAT'S OWNER WILL RECOGNIZE HIM.
WELL, ANYWAY, I HATE THAT PEOPLE WOULD DO THIS. SO AFTERWARD, I FOLLOWED THE GUY WITH MY MOPED.
YOU'RE CRAZY! THAT COULD'VE BEEN DANGEROUS.
NO WORRIES, I DIDN'T EVEN GET LOST. AND I SAW WHO HE WAS GIVING THE BAG TO.
THAT'S IMPOSSIBLE! I DON'T UNDERSTAND ANYTHING!
I CAN'T BELIEVE IT.

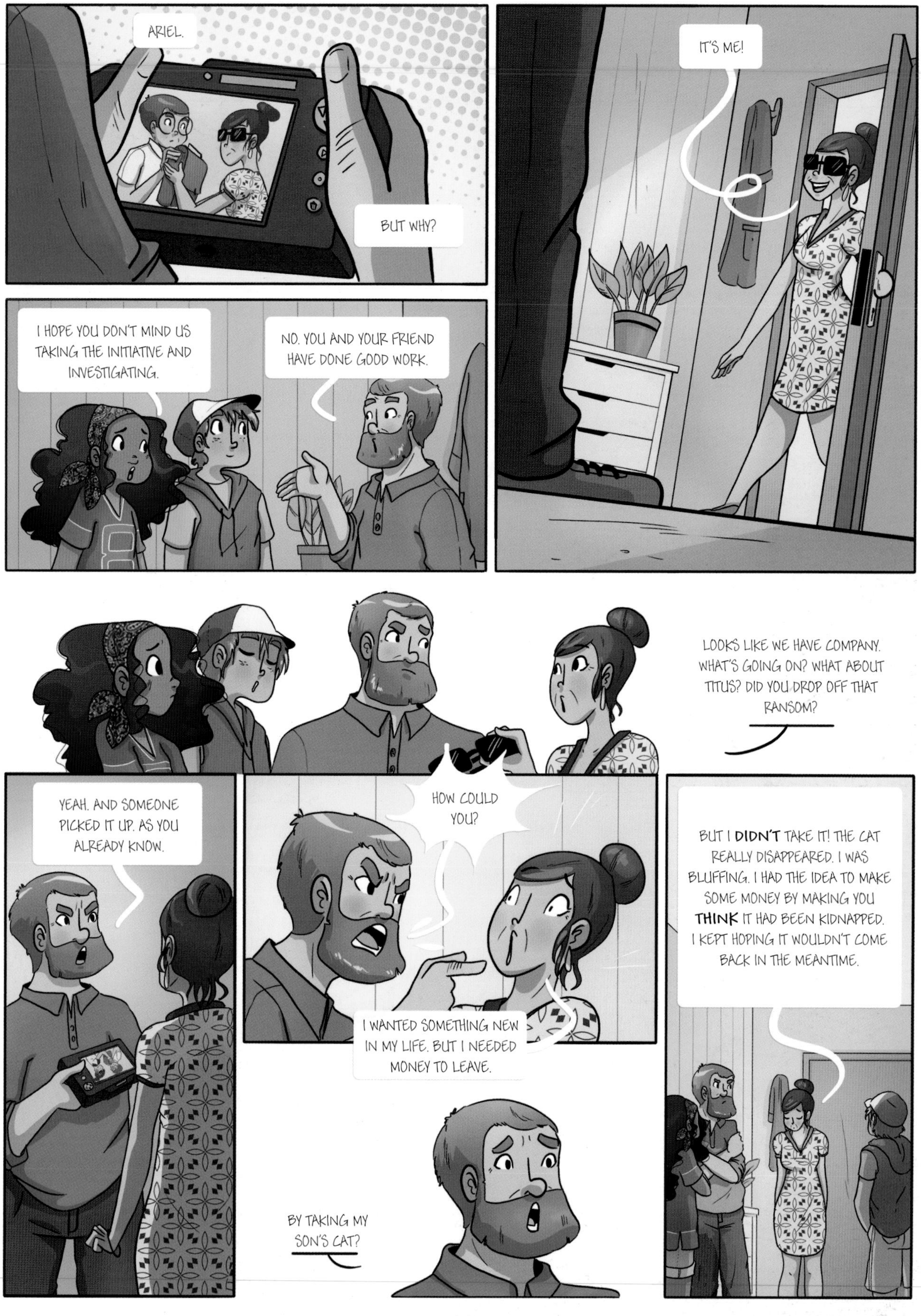
ARIEL.
BUT WHY?
IT'S ME!
I HOPE YOU DON'T MIND US TAKING THE INITIATIVE AND INVESTIGATING.
NO. YOU AND YOUR FRIEND HAVE DONE GOOD WORK.
LOOKS LIKE WE HAVE COMPANY. WHAT'S GOING ON? WHAT ABOUT TITUS? DID YOU DROP OFF THAT RANSOM?
YEAH. AND SOMEONE PICKED IT UP. AS YOU ALREADY KNOW.
HOW COULD YOU?
I WANTED SOMETHING NEW IN MY LIFE. BUT I NEEDED MONEY TO LEAVE.
BY TAKING MY SON'S CAT?
BUT I DIDN'T TAKE IT! THE CAT REALLY DISAPPEARED. I WAS BLUFFING. I HAD THE IDEA TO MAKE SOME MONEY BY MAKING YOU THINK IT HAD BEEN KIDNAPPED. I KEPT HOPING IT WOULDN'T COME BACK IN THE MEANTIME.

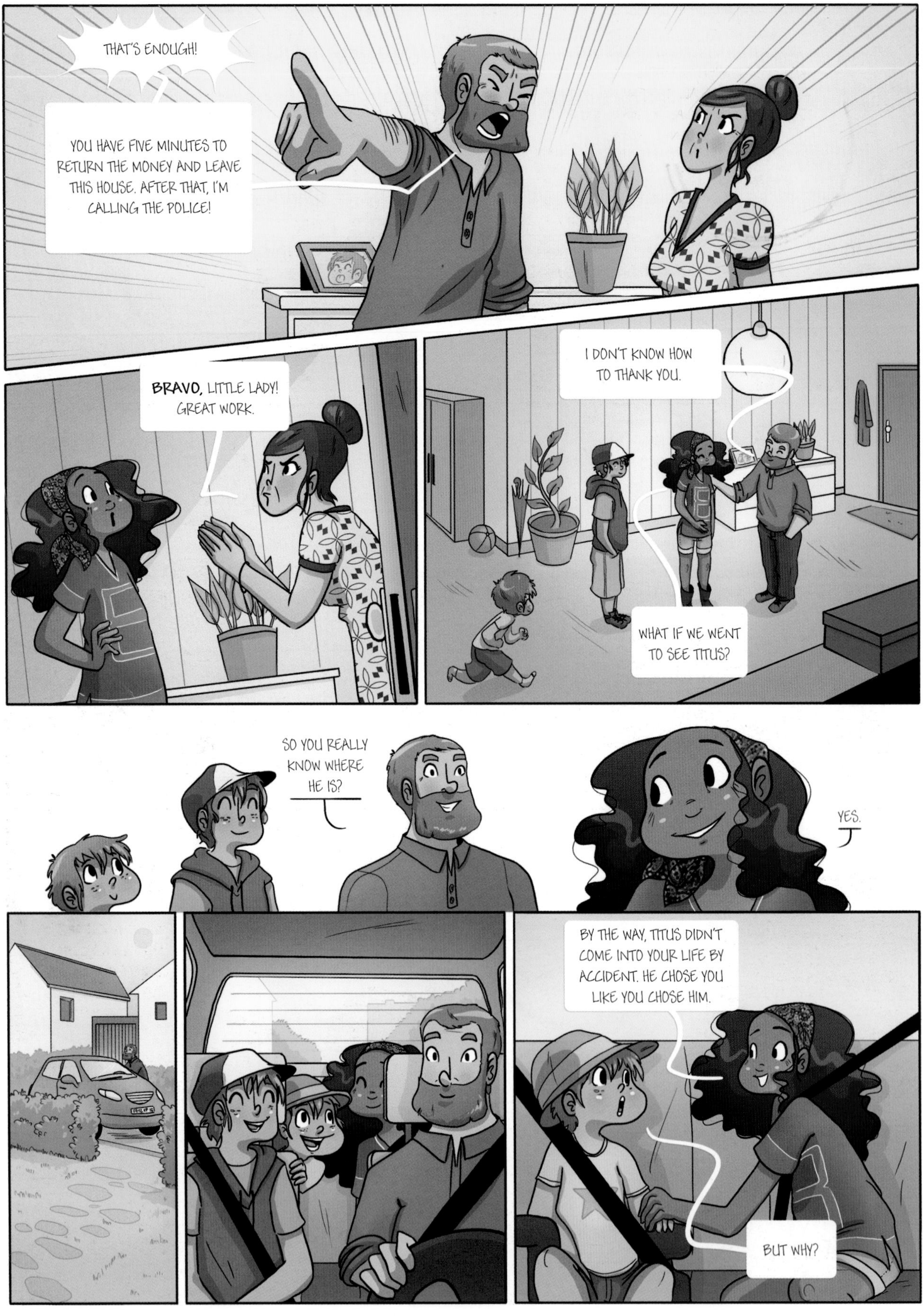
THAT'S ENOUGH!
YOU HAVE FIVE MINUTES TO RETURN THE MONEY AND LEAVE THIS HOUSE. AFTER THAT, I'M CALLING THE POLICE!
BRAVO, LITTLE LADY! GREAT WORK.
I DON'T KNOW HOW TO THANK YOU.
WHAT IF WE WENT TO SEE TITUS?
SO YOU REALLY KNOW WHERE HE IS?
YES.
BY THE WAY, TITUS DIDN'T COME INTO YOUR LIFE BY ACCIDENT. HE CHOSE YOU LIKE YOU CHOSE HIM.
BUT WHY?

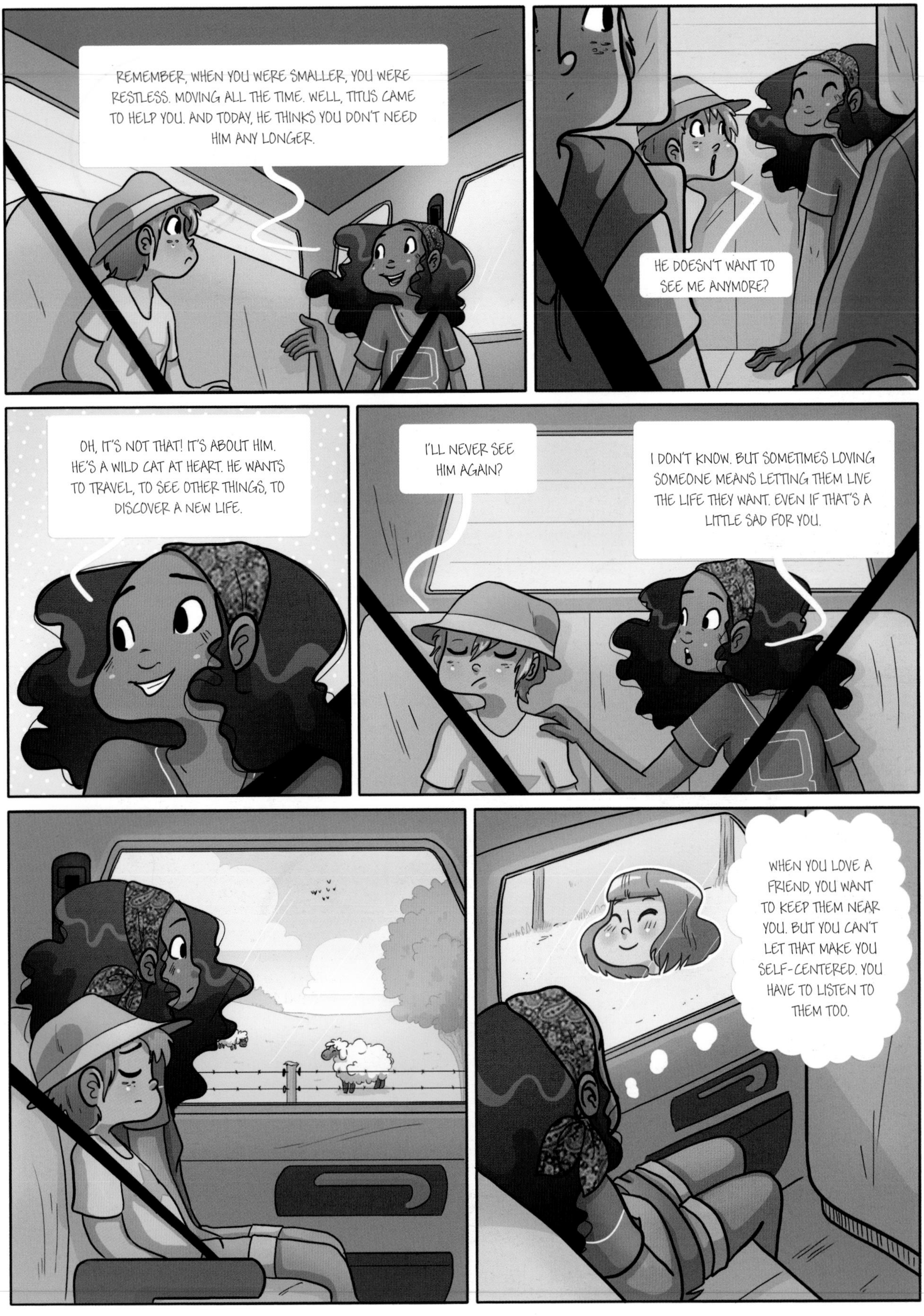
REMEMBER, WHEN YOU WERE SMALLER, YOU WERE RESTLESS. MOVING ALL THE TIME. WELL, TITUS CAME TO HELP YOU. AND TODAY, HE THINKS YOU DON'T NEED HIM ANY LONGER.
HE DOESN'T WANT TO SEE ME ANYMORE?
OH, IT'S NOT THAT! IT'S ABOUT HIM. HE'S A WILD CAT AT HEART. HE WANTS TO TRAVEL, TO SEE OTHER THINGS, TO DISCOVER A NEW LIFE.
I'LL NEVER SEE HIM AGAIN?
I DON'T KNOW. BUT SOMETIMES LOVING SOMEONE MEANS LETTING THEM LIVE THE LIFE THEY WANT. EVEN IF THAT'S A LITTLE SAD FOR YOU.
WHEN YOU LOVE A FRIEND, YOU WANT TO KEEP THEM NEAR YOU. BUT YOU CAN'T LET THAT MAKE YOU SELF-CENTERED. YOU HAVE TO LISTEN TO THEM TOO.

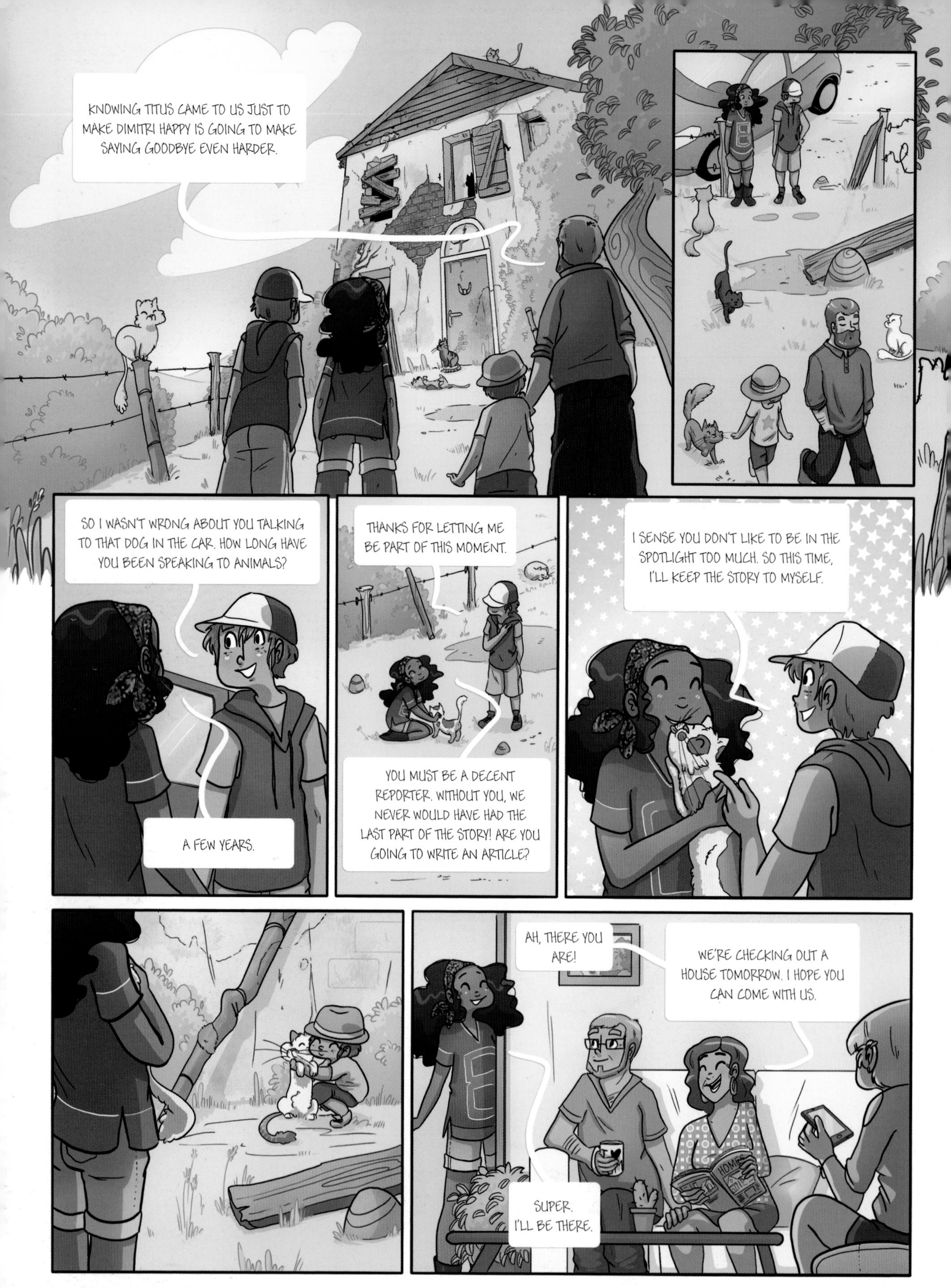

KNOWING TITUS CAME TO US JUST TO MAKE DIMITRI HAPPY IS GOING TO MAKE SAYING GOODBYE EVEN HARDER.
SO I WASN'T WRONG ABOUT YOU TALKING TO THAT DOG IN THE CAR. HOW LONG HAVE YOU BEEN SPEAKING TO ANIMALS?
A FEW YEARS.
THANKS FOR LETTING ME BE PART OF THIS MOMENT.
YOU MUST BE A DECENT REPORTER. WITHOUT YOU, WE NEVER WOULD HAVE HAD THE LAST PART OF THE STORY! ARE YOU GOING TO WRITE AN ARTICLE?
I SENSE YOU DON'T LIKE TO BE IN THE SPOTLIGHT TOO MUCH. SO THIS TIME, I'LL KEEP THE STORY TO MYSELF.
AH, THERE YOU ARE!
WE'RE CHECKING OUT A HOUSE TOMORROW. I HOPE YOU CAN COME WITH US.
SUPER. I'LL BE THERE.

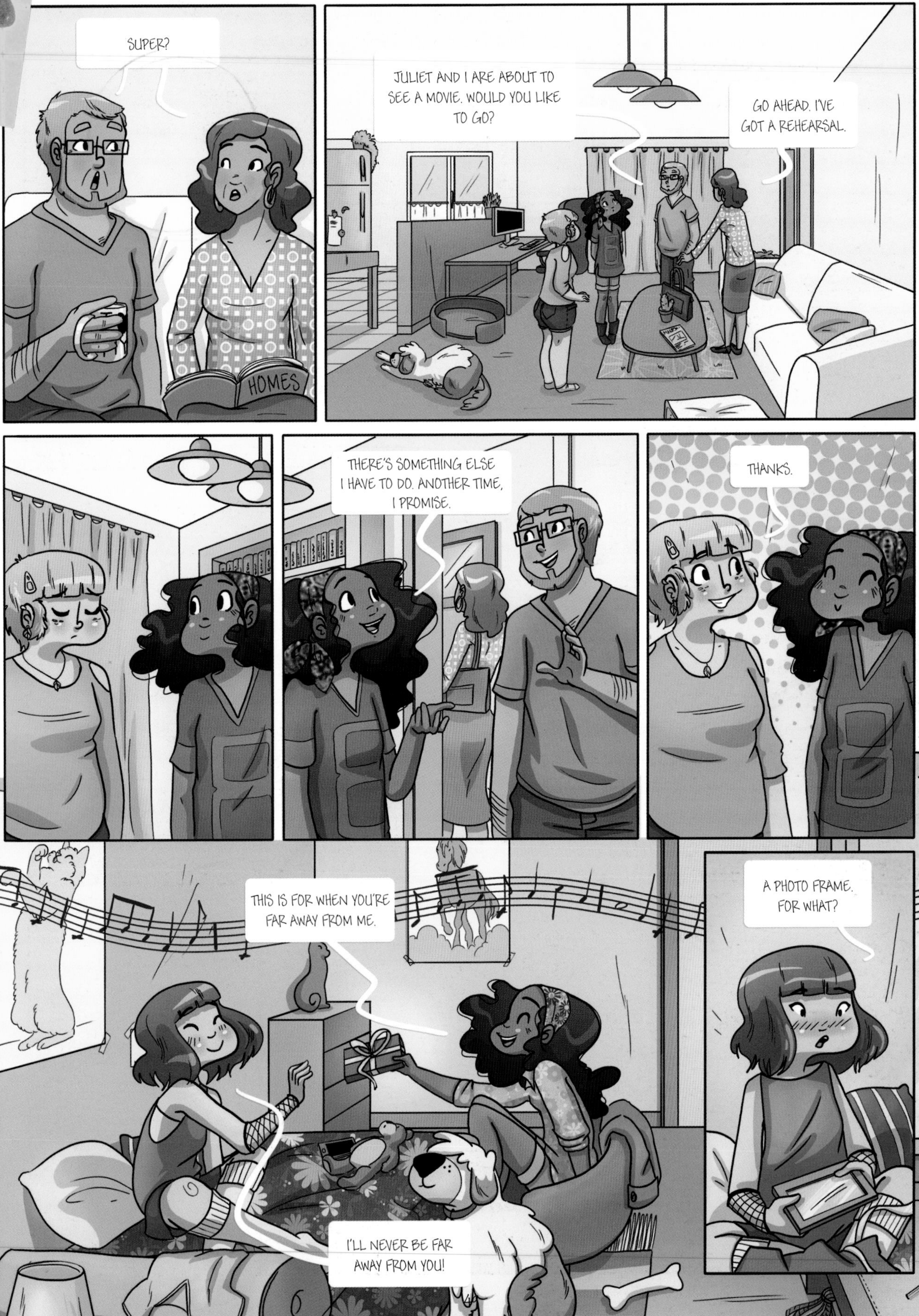
SUPER?
JULIET AND I ARE ABOUT TO SEE A MOVIE. WOULD YOU LIKE TO GO?
GO AHEAD. I'VE GOT A REHEARSAL.
HOMES
THERE'S SOMETHING ELSE I HAVE TO DO. ANOTHER TIME, I PROMISE.
THANKS.
THIS IS FOR WHEN YOU'RE FAR AWAY FROM ME.
I'LL NEVER BE FAR AWAY FROM YOU!
A PHOTO FRAME. FOR WHAT?

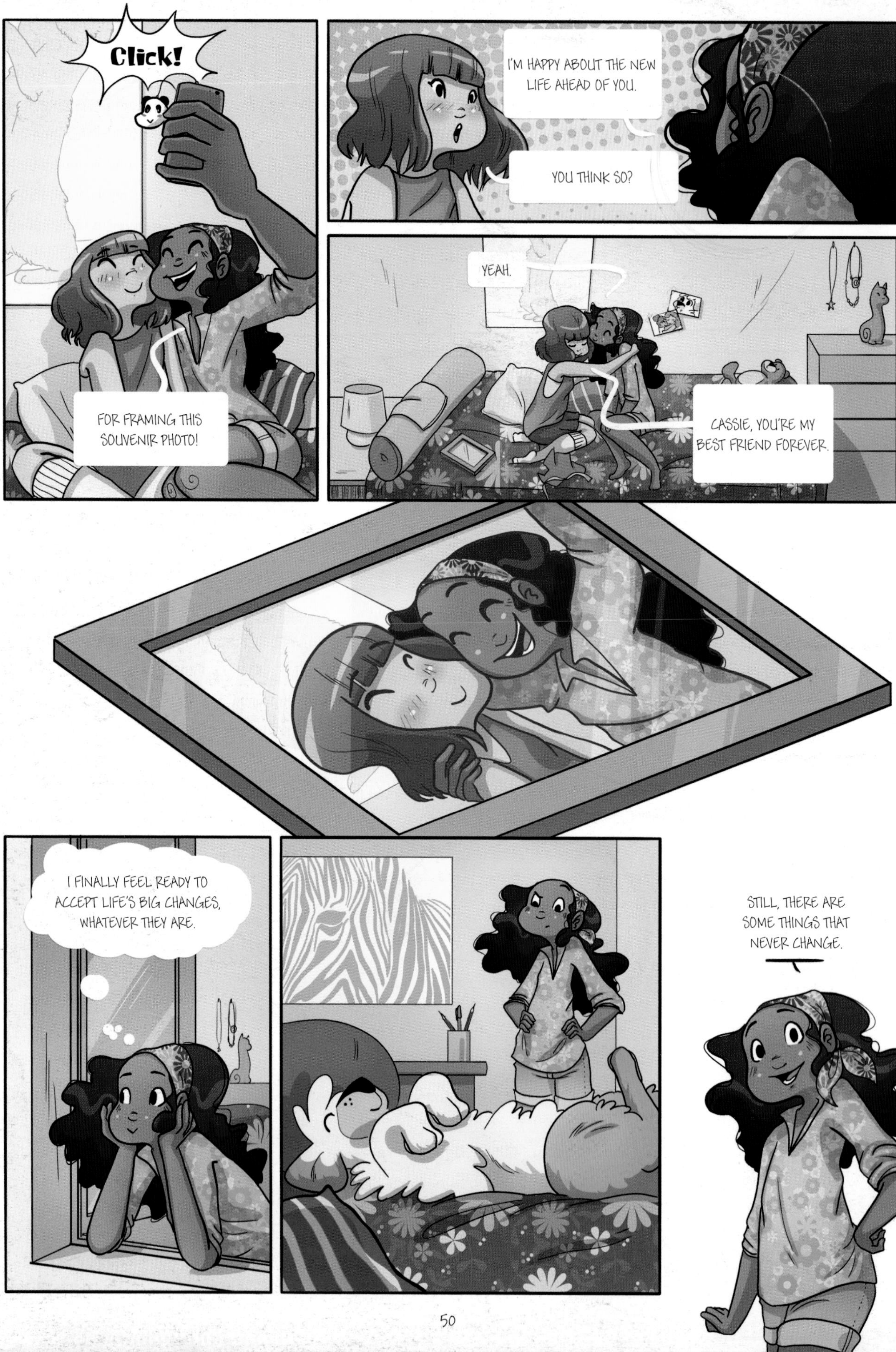
Click!
FOR FRAMING THIS SOUVENIR PHOTO!
I'M HAPPY ABOUT THE NEW LIFE AHEAD OF YOU.
YOU THINK SO?
YEAH.
CASSIE, YOU'RE MY BEST FRIEND FOREVER.
I FINALLY FEEL READY TO ACCEPT LIFE'S BIG CHANGES, WHATEVER THEY ARE.
STILL, THERE ARE SOME THINGS THAT NEVER CHANGE.

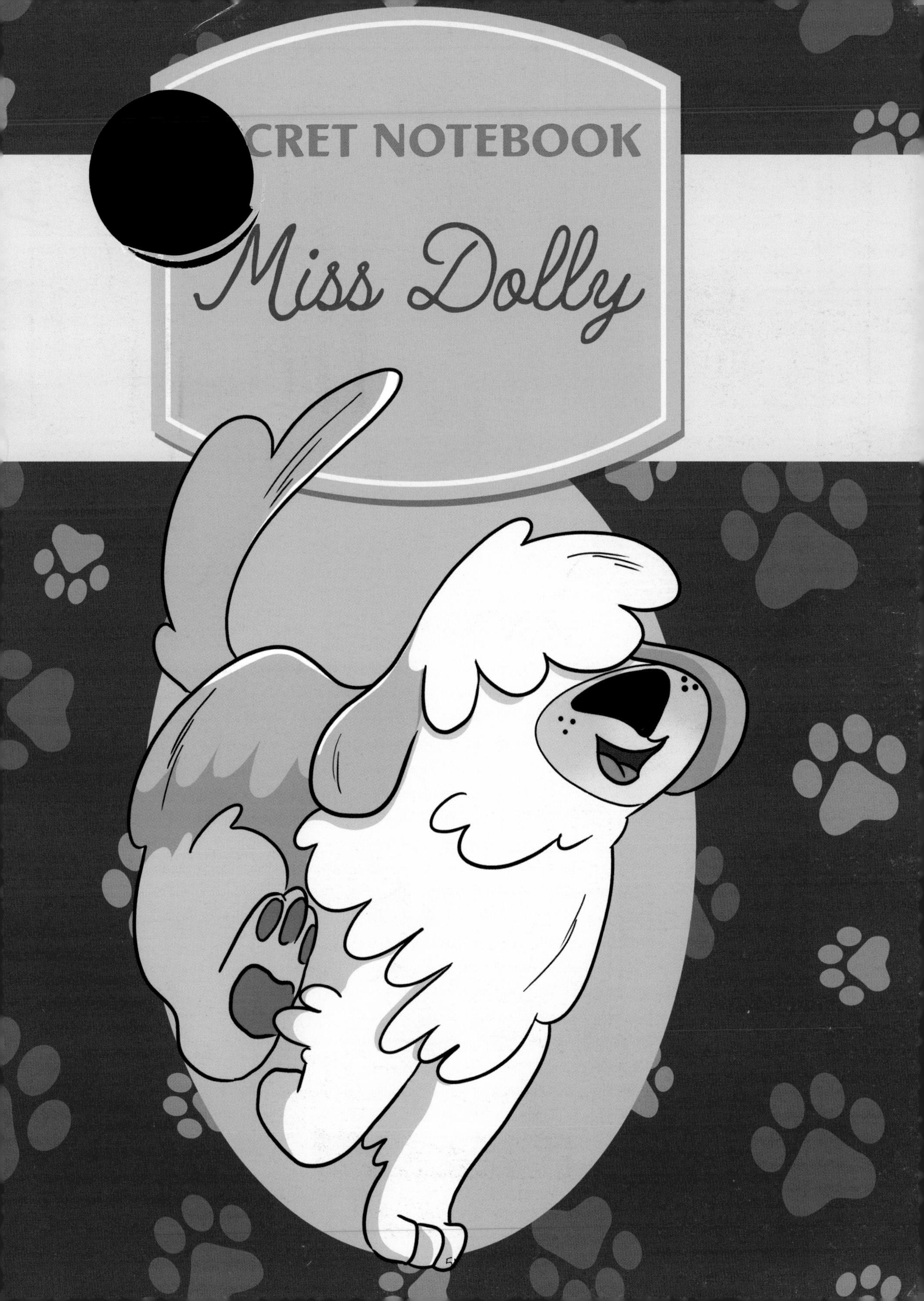
CRET NOTEBOOK
Miss Dolly

Memories, memories . . .

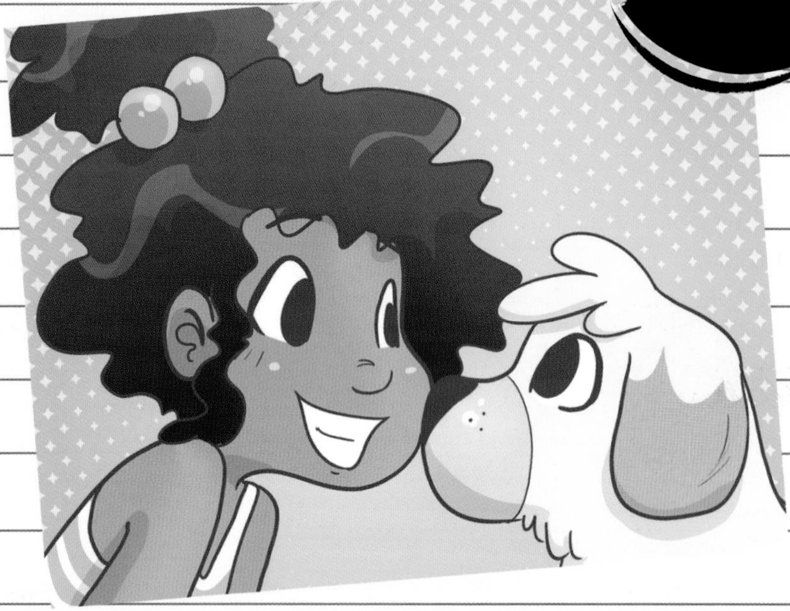

HOW I MET MISS DOLLY:

When I turned ten, Mom surprised me by taking me to a shelter so we could adopt a dog. I went crazy with joy! I'd been waiting for this day for so long. It had always been my dream to have a dog!

***

I couldn't wait to meet the pooch who was going to be my new friend. While almost all the puppies greeted me with some happy woofs, Miss Dolly was the only one to completely ignore me. She kept lying in her corner, folded in on herself, sighing long sighs. She looked so sad and miserable that my sensitive heart couldn't resist. THAT'S HOW SHE WON ME OVER, HANDS DOWN!

Who's this?

Miss Dolly has a big bobtail.

She's an English shepherd.

This bobtailed shepherd is very

sociable. She gets along with everyone.

She's a big friend of the kids!

She's also a good sport whenever

I put her hair up.

No joke!

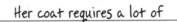

Her coat requires a lot of

maintenance and grooming.

Decoding Miss Dolly's behavior

 WARNING! This is the look of a dog that has made a big mistake. Better ~~run fast!~~

 This look says you have something Miss Dolly wants, like ice cream or a hot dog. Ignore it!

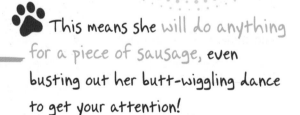 This means she will do anything for a piece of sausage, even busting out her butt-wiggling dance to get your attention!

 When a dog sleeps on its side, that means it feels cozy in its space. She can relax and sleep because she's comfortable. Thank you, my Dolly!

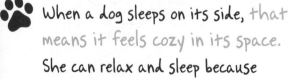

Miss Dolly,
the Queen of Goofiness!

This dog lives in the moment. If I catch her doing something naughty, I scold her. But if I'm not sure when the naughtiness happened, I let her be. Miss Dolly wouldn't understand why I'm scolding her because she already would have forgotten what she did.

When Miss Dolly was a puppy, sometimes she would pee inside. To show her little by little what was good and what was bad, if I took her out and she did her business, I'd reward her with a little treat. Miss Dolly understood really quickly:

peeing inside = we have a problem

peeing outside = you get a snack

About the Author

Isabelle Bottier

Isabelle Bottier is a writer based in Ile-de-France, France. She made her debut writing for French television and quickly began to write on several animated series. She also uses her imagination to create comics for young readers.

About the Artist

Hélène Canac

Hélène Canac lives in the sanctuary of comics, Angoulême, France. She has studied graphic design, publishing, and advertising, and she worked in animation after her time as a student. She also works in youth illustration, providing art for novels, games, notebooks . . . and, most recently, comics!

Coming soon:
the second Cassandra:
Animal Psychic graphic novel,
Out on a Limb!